Corked

By

Lynda L. Lock

&

your friend Sparky

Dedication

In loving memory of my best friend and adventure partner, Lawrie Lock.

We crammed a lot of escapades into 39 years of love and laughter.

Yazmin Guzmán Rivera

1982 – 2020

I'm frequently asked if my friend Yazmin Guzmán Rivera is the role model for my fictional character Yasmin Medina in my novels. The answer is yes, and no. When I first started writing, I asked Yazmin if I could name one of my characters, who was a Mexicana with curly hair, Yasmin (spelled with an s).

The character Yasmin Medina isn't nearly as adventurous as Yazmin Guzmán Rivera but she is as pretty and as kind and she has a zest for life. The real Yazmin said my character could have been she when she was younger and shyer. I chuckled at the thought of Yazmin Guzmán Rivera ever being shy.

Fly high Warrior Woman. You are missed.

Foreword:

The Royal Canadian Mounted Police, RCMP, is the federal force that has policed most of Canada since February 1, 1920, although some Canadian provinces and many of the larger cities now have their own police services.

The Okanagan Valley in British Columbia, Canada, where this story is set, is policed by the RCMP, whose ranks and titles can be a long and cumbersome mouthful of words. For example, the local 'top cop' is responsible for a vast area as the Detachment Commander of Penticton Okanagan Similkameen Regional Detachment. I have shortened the formal ranks to something more manageable where possible.

Since many of my readers are American, I have switched from writing my novels in British English to American English, which creates a challenge with the ranks for the RCMP. Sergeant is the correct spelling for an RCMP officer in Canada, but the common nickname for the rank would be Sarge.

One of the minor characters, Sergeant William Williams, is a Non-Commissioned Officer, NCO. Therefore, he would be addressed as Sarge, or boss, or depending on his relationship with his subordinates, perhaps by his first name. He would not be addressed as sir. That is for commissioned officers, those who receive their commission from the monarch, like the military ranks.

Clear as mud? I hope so.

Cheers, Lynda

Chapter 1

No Regrets Winery Okanagan Valley

The loneliness of the empty winery huddled against her. It was well past closing time and the other staff had left hours ago, calling their goodnights and Happy Valentine's Day wishes as they jostled out the door, leaving her and the company president, Kingsley Quartermain, toiling over a mountain of paperwork. The spring release of the new white wines and the shareholders' dinner were scheduled mid-March and Quartermain had asked her to stay late to help him sort out a few things before the event.

Two days ago, a polar vortex bringing sub-zero temperatures had settled over the valley and the single electric heater in her office struggled to keep the room habitable. Shivering she spun her wheeled chair to face the heater and propped her feet on top. *God, I'm freezing.* She'd give anything to be at home in her apartment, snuggled close to her gas fireplace, a glass of Cab Sauv in her hand. *Happy Valentine's Day to me*, she dryly mused. No cat, no dog, and no love interest. Not even a goldfish to greet her when came home.

Corked

Kingsley unlocked a drawer on his desk, pulled out a thick file and dropped it with a thump on her desk. She flinched at the noise. He flipped the cover open, revealing copies of share certificates in denominations of twenty-five thousand dollars.

"Make a spreadsheet for these," he directed.

An hour later she said, "This is very odd, Kingsley. Our share subscription seems to be oversold," she held the printout in her hand. "I show over two hundred percent of the shares sold."

He laughed, a deep knowing laugh. A laugh without anxiety, or unease, or concern. His large brown eyes trapped hers. "What about it?" he asked, his solid frame looming over her desk.

A ripple of apprehension skittered up her spine. *Don't be a fool; this is Kingsley. He wouldn't harm you,* she admonished herself.

Yet, she felt exposed. Unprotected. The bitter February night pressed its face against the windows trying to peer past the gloom into the illuminated office. The building was located on an expansive acreage, pushed up against a rocky bluff, on a private road. In the winter no one came this way after sundown.

Stay calm. "Won't someone notice?" She asked lightly.

"The shareholders are sheep," he replied. "They'll believe anything I tell them. It's the romance of the wine industry," he said making air quotes. "They willingly hand over their savings or their children's education funds, or put a second mortgage on their house just to be able to brag to their friends: 'I'm an owner of a winery,'" he mocked.

"You're the boss," she replied. Despite his distasteful comments, she kept her expression carefully neutral. The industry was populated by notable celebrities who were either passively or actively involved in the business, everything from hockey players, to golfers, and prominent Hollywood actors. A smaller number of wineries, like this one, were owned by a consortium of shareholders. Quartermain's disdain for his financial backers was appalling.

"Exactly, and only two people know about this," he said, leaning over to make eye contact. "Just you, and me," he said pointing at her, then himself. "It's our little secret, Ellen. You understand?"

"Yes, of course," Ellen Taylor agreed, her stomach clenching with anger and fear. Why had he involved her? He was capable of creating his own spreadsheet. She didn't need to know that he was scamming the investors. *What was he up to?*

"It's late. Let's call it a night," he said.

"Sounds good," she said, shutting down the computer and reaching for her purse.

His broad hand lightly encircled her wrist. A smile creased his cheeks, but it failed to reach his eyes. "Take a nice bottle of red home for your dinner, Ellen. You've earned it," he said.

"Thank you, but that's not necessary," she replied, slowly lowering her arm to her side until he released his grip.

"I insist," he said, and his eyes commanded.

"All right, thank you, Kingsley. That's very thoughtful." She pushed her chair back and stood with one hand on her desk to support her weight, an attempt to hide her vibrating knees. The sensation of being stalked by a cougar waiting for the perfect moment to pounce itched at her spine as she walked with careful deliberation to the coat rack. She pulled on her heavy winter jacket, leaving her gloves and hat stuffed in the pockets, and scurried out. The icy wind nipped painfully at her uncovered fingers and ears as she scrambled to unlock her Mazda hatchback.

Alone in her apartment, she leaned against the wooden door that until yesterday had been solid and comforting. Now, it appeared to be flimsy and easily shattered with one solid kick to the handle. She dragged a heavy armchair across the room and shoved it against the door. Teeth chattering with the cold and fear, she moved the thermostat up a few degrees.

Working with Kingsley and learning the wine industry had been, until now, fascinating. He had always been affable, smiling, and persuasive in a genial manner. This was a side of his character that she had not experienced before. She felt threatened, afraid. The menace in his eyes had been unmistakable. Don't question — *just do as I say*.

Her hand shook as she uncorked the bottle. The neck clattered against the rim of her glass as she poured a sizeable amount. With one hand on the kitchen counter to steady herself, she tipped back the wine and swallowed a mouthful. *What should I do?* She checked the time on her phone: ten-thirty.

With trembling hands, she searched her contact list for Daniel Cooper, an accountant at the firm that handled the winery's finances. Punching in the number, she put the phone to her ear and listened to the call ring through.

"Hello?" asked a sleepy voice.

"Hi, Daniel, it's me, Ellen."

"It's late." He stifled a yawn. "Everything okay?"

"No, not really," she said. "I'm worried and scared." Ellen sucked in large mouthful as she listened to him getting out of bed.

"It's work, honey. Go back to sleep," she heard Daniel say to his wife. "I'm going to take this call in the living room."

Ellen gulped another soothing mouthful of wine as she listened to him pad to the living room, then snap on a light, and settle on a piece of furniture. "Okay, tell me what's going on." She heard him stifle another yawn.

"I'm so sorry to wake you up, but I didn't know what else to do," she said, then described the events of the evening and the discrepancy in the share subscriptions. Kingsley's behavior. Her fear. "Am I over-reacting?" she asked her friend.

"God no. What he's done is illegal, extremely illegal," Daniel sputtered.

"That's what I thought. I don't want to be accused of being involved in his scam."

"Unfortunately, Ellen, you are going to be suspected until we can sort it out."

"You'll have to do an audit, but then he'll know that I blew the whistle on him," she moaned.

"Go to work tomorrow, and act natural. I'll discuss this with my partners."

"I've never seen him act like this before. It worries me," Ellen said. "How on earth does he think he will get away with defrauding the investors this way?"

"Maybe he thinks he can bluff his way through the meeting, Daniel said. "Just go to work and behave as if nothing is wrong. I'll figure this out, trust me."

Chapter 2

Isla Mujeres

"Good morning, sexy," Jessica Sanderson leaned over and kissed Mike Lyons. "Coffee?" Her long blond mane spilled over her suntanned shoulders, brushing against his face as her lips fastened on his. It was hard to believe that she and Mike had been living together for just six days. They were so comfortable with each other it felt as if they had been together for months if not years.

"Mmmm, yum," he said as he disengaged his lips. "Coffee would be excellent."

She flipped off the covers, dropped her feet to the tile floor, and pulled a t-shirt on over her head. "Ten minutes and I shall return with your coffee, sir," she deadpanned. "Come on Sparky, pee and poops." Padding barefoot to the kitchen, she knew Mike was watching her, checking her ass. She opened her back door, giving Sparky, her short-legged Mexi-mutt, access to her compact but securely fenced yard and then switched on the coffeemaker. Mike had a great butt too, muscular, not skinny. Some men were just too thin. She didn't want a lover whose behind was smaller than hers.

While she waited for the coffee to brew, Jessica refreshed the shallow dish of water on her kitchen counter for Geek the Gecko, the tiny lizard who lived behind her refrigerator. In exchange for his bug catching abilities, she gave him drinking water and a safe place to live. She occasionally pulled out the refrigerator to sweep up his droppings. *A servant to both a gecko and a pooch.*

"What are you going to do, Geek?" Jessica asked, aiming her question in the general direction of the gecko's hiding place. "We're going to California and we might not return to Isla."

Geek refrained from chirping back an answer. Perhaps he was annoyed that she was abandoning him, or maybe he'd already packed his bags and moved. If he had relocated outside, he would have easy access to food and water. Her eyes strayed to her front door: There was a gecko-sized gap under both her front and the back doors. He'd be fine, but she was going to miss her interactions with the little lizard. But then, leaving her cozy *casa* and her friends, especially her friends, was difficult too.

Sparky trotted back into the kitchen as the coffeemaker sputtered its last gasp of hot water into the carafe. Jessica filled two cups about three-quarters full then she added milk to the frother and switched it on. The appliance whirred and whipped the milk into a hot frenzy of foam, then she shared it between the two cups, adding a drizzle of caramel. Her best friend Yasmin had hooked her on drinking coffee like this. Frilly coffee is what she called it.

Mike was propped up in bed, flipping through various news pages on his phone. "Have you been keeping up with the stories about a weird virus that has popped up in China? Coronavirus?"

"Nope. I hate reading the news. It's always depressing." She set the coffees on her nightstand and climbed onto the bed, handing Mike his cup once she was settled.

Mike's green eyes flicked a question at her: "Really? You don't keep up with the news?"

"Nope. The same gloomy stories are repeated over and over and over on all of the 24-hour news stations. If it's important someone will tell me what's going on." She nodded at him, "And I'm guessing you are about to."

"Yep," he said, "let me read this to you. December 31st 2019 the Wuhan Municipal Health Commission, China, reported a cluster of cases of pneumonia in Wuhan, Hubei Province, but no deaths. A novel coronavirus was eventually identified. January 5th the World Health Organization publicized the outbreak though conventional news outlets and on social media."

Corked

Mike paused, sipped his coffee, glanced at Jessica to see if she was still listening to him and then resumed reading the news article to her, "January 30th, the World Health Organization reported 7,818 total confirmed cases worldwide, with the majority of these in China, and 82 cases reported in 18 countries outside China. The World Health Organization gave a risk assessment of very high for China, and high at the global level."

Jessica peered at him over the top of her cup, "And? How does that affect us?" She patted the bed. Sparky jumped up and flipped into the tummy-up position. She ran her hand over the thin white hair covering his black and pink spotted stomach, rubbed his chest and scratched under his chin. It was odd how the hair on his underside was thin, straight, and white, while his back was covered with thick curly hair, in a tweedy mix of gray, white, and black. His dark raccoon-style mask and long brown ears accented his unusual and intriguing eyes. He had white around his brown irises, like a human.

"Well, it doesn't, yet. But it could be another epidemic like SARS, or the swine flu."

"We aren't traveling to China. We're only going to the Sonoma Valley in California, so it's not my problem," She said popping up one shoulder in an unconcerned shrug and continued, "I have more important things to think about getting ready to leave Isla. So far, I've worked my last shift at *Loco*

Lobo. I've packed my stuff. Yasmin is taking my golf cart *Frita Bandita*. All I have left to do is say goodbye to my friends." She tucked her chin hoping Mike wouldn't see the tears caught in the corner of her eyes and threatening to drip into her coffee.

Mike set aside his phone, "Jess, are you having second thoughts about coming to California with me?"

Jessica peeked at Mike and saw his uncertainty, his worry. "No, not at all. I thrive on new experiences. I'm just sad that I am leaving my friends. Weird right?"

"No, definitely not weird. I get it. You've lived and worked on the island for almost five years and you've got some very close personal bonds with Yasmin, Carlos, Diego, Cristina, Pedro and Maricruz, to name a few," he said, handing her a tissue. "I just want you to know I'm not pressuring you."

Jessica put her mug on the nightstand, wiped her eyes, and wriggled further into the bed. She turned and brushed her hand over his short beard. Her eyes softened and locked on his. "I'm looking forward to our new adventure and learning about the industry. And exploring the wineries of the Sonoma Valley."

"If you're sure," Mike said as she touched his face. "That makes me very happy."

"Good," she said, swallowing a mouthful of coffee. "Now, about tonight ..."

"Tonight?"

"Yes, our hasta luego bash at *Loco Lobo Restaurante*. Sparky is invited too."

"Oh hell, I forgot," Mike said, "but, since Sparky is invited, I guess we had better put in an appearance."

"*Si*, they love him. I think everyone will miss my dog more than me."

"No chance," Mike said, leaning in to smooch her. "What time tonight?"

"Seven-ish, *mas o menos*, more or less," she answered.

"So, probably nine or ten Mexican-time before anyone actually gets there," Mike quipped.

"Most of our friends will dribble in at various times, but we're the guests of honor so we have to be on time," Jessica said. An invitation to an event, or a party, or even a wedding, might say six in the evening but most of the guests probably wouldn't arrive until at least two hours later. It wasn't rude to be late, it was the custom. Recently she had been invited to a birthday party and had arrived an hour past the stated time, only to find the hosts still in the shower when she knocked on their door. They had greeted her good-naturedly, teased her

Corked

for arriving too early, and put her to work hanging the party decorations.

"I feel awkward just hanging around waiting for people to show up."

"The food and drinks are on Carlos and Yasmin, so you can entertain yourself that way."

"You smooth talker." Mike held out his coffee cup. "Any chance of a refill in exchange for more kisses?" He lifted one eyebrow.

"Wait." She pushed gently on his chest, "I get the coffee and you get more kisses? How is that an even trade?"

"You get kisses too," he answered, hopefully puckering his lips.

Chapter 3

Isla Mujeres

"Quiet everyone! I'd like to propose a toast!" shouted Diego Avalos.

Carlos Mendoza, the owner and Jessica's boss at *Loco Lobo Restaurante*, put two fingers in his lips and blew a shrill blast. *"¡Silencio!"* he bellowed, and the background chatter abated to a manageable level.

The restaurant was closed to the public for the event but Carlos had left the rolldown metal shutters open to let the crowd spill out onto Hidalgo Avenue. Every restaurant proprietor on the street was permitted to use part of the pedestrian walkway for additional tables and chairs. It created a chaotic and sociable atmosphere for tourists who strolled the avenue, reading menus and listening to the mariachis before deciding on where they would dine, or in this case space for the large and noisy collection of well-wishers to find more elbow room.

"Gracias," Diego said, as the group quietened down. He reached over and wrapped his arm around Jessica. "I think we're all looking

forward to a big drop in the crime rate on our little island when Jessica leaves tomorrow," he said. "Unfortunately, the people of California have no idea of the mayhem this one woman can create." Diego raised his glass. "To the rapid departure of Jessica and Sparky. And our deepest condolences to Mike."

"Uff," Diego exhaled when Jessica jabbed him in the ribs with her elbow.

"*¡Pendejo!*" She scoffed.

Diego tossed his head back and roared with laughter. "Oh god, I am going to miss you, *hermanita*."

"Likewise, *hermano*, but I'll come back to visit … frequently."

Holding up his hands to ward off the suggestion, Diego sputtered, "*Por favor*, not too often. Trouble follows you."

Jessica lifted her chin and glared up at Diego's off-center nose, his wide smile, and dark brown eyes. "If you don't quit with the derogatory remarks, I won't leave. I'll tell Mike that I've changed my mind. That my friends need me here on Isla."

Diego wrapped her in a tight hug. "You know we'll miss you, and me in particular. You're as close to me as a baby sister," he said.

"Stop it. You're making me cry." She sniffed and swiped a hand under her nose.

"What time tomorrow do you leave?"

"On the noon boat. Why?" she asked.

"Cristina wants to bring our brood of brats to wave goodbye."

"You know that's going to make me cry again, right?"

"*Si*, me too." He kissed the top of her head and released her with a little push into the crowded restaurant. "Go, mingle. Say goodbye to everyone."

Jessica stood on tiptoe and spotted Mike. His thinning hair allowed the overhead lighting to reflect off of his sexy skull. She loved that about him: He was comfortable in his own skin and didn't try to hide his baldness under a ghastly comb-over.

Mike was tucked into a corner, deep in conversation with Pedro Velazquez and naval lieutenant Maricruz Zapata. He was fine for now. She turned to smile at the person beside her, Yasmin Medina de Mendoza, her *Loco Lobo* workmate, friend, and partner in their escapades. Their boss, Carlos Mendoza had finally got the nerve to ask Yasmin to marry him and their first anniversary was next week, right in the middle of the annual five days of Carnaval festivities.

"Damn," Jessica turned to her friend, "I just realized we won't be here for either your anniversary or Carnaval this year."

"No, you won't be but tomorrow is the start of your new adventure with Mike," Yasmin said. She wrapped Jessica in a hug. "I'm going to miss you, so much."

"Me too, but we can FaceTime regularly." Jessica disengaged and studied her best friend. The woman was fricking beautiful: deep green eyes, masses of dark curly hair, and a wide generous smile that beamed joy and love into the world. Leaving Yasmin was like tearing out a piece of her heart and tossing it on the ground to be trampled by others.

"*Si*, we can, but it won't be the same."

"I know," Jessica agreed, "but now that you are a respectable married woman who is trying to start a family, it's a good thing I'm leaving and can't drag you into anymore dangerous escapades."

"Being a responsible grownup is overrated," Yasmin said. "Besides, you didn't include me in the recent murder investigation, involving the wealthy Nashville socialite and her very dead musician husband. I feel snubbed."

Jessica snorted a laugh at that last comment. "Mike and I didn't intend to snub you," she said. "I feel a bit badly for Mike. He spent a bundle on VIP packages for him and me, but of the four days of events I only got to see the one act, Brandon Forbes, the guy who died."

Yasmin nodded that she had heard, then shifted aside to let Carlos pull Jessica into a hug. He bussed her cheek.

Jessica smiled affectionately at the man who had started off as their boss, and had become one of her closest friends. She lightly touched a spot just above his ear. "You're getting distinguished looking, boss."

"That's just a polite way of saying I'm over forty and I look old," he quipped.

"A few years past forty," she corrected, "but, the thick dark hair with a little touch of gray at the temples looks good on you," she said, then added, "I thought Mayas didn't normally turn gray when they aged."

"It's my mixed blood," he said, then changed the subject. "What're we going to do for excitement when you're gone?"

"Have a nice, quiet, normal life producing pretty babies with your beautiful wife?" Jessica quipped.

Carlos shot a look at Yasmin, "You told her?"

Corked

"*Si*, I told Jessica we're trying to get pregnant."

"About that," Carlos said, "how do we," he jogged a finger back and forth between Yasmin and himself, "how do we get pregnant? As far as I know only females are fitted with the right equipment and are brave enough to produce babies."

Jessica bounced her eyebrows at Yasmin. "Good question," she said. "You can answer that one."

"It's just a feel-good expression to make the daddies believe they are sharing the experience," Yasmin said.

"So, I'm the lucky sperm donor, you do all the hard stuff and I get half of the credit?" Carlos asked, "Is that how it works?"

"*Si*," Yasmin agreed.

"Sweet!"

"It also entitles you to equal time feeding and changing the baby," she added, "including the middle of the night."

"But I don't have the right equipment," he said, pointing at his impressive chest.

"There is a new invention called a baby bottle," Yasmin squeezed his forearm and crinkled her nose, "I'll teach you how to use it, *mi amor*."

Chapter 4

Isla Mujeres

"Well, I'll be damned," Mike grunted. He stared at the screen on his phone then typed in a short reply.

"What?" Jessica asked. She patted her travel bag, checking for the umpteenth time that she had packed the documents, then reached for the handle on her suitcase. They were ahead of schedule for the boat but it was better to get there early. February was high season and the boats were spilling over with tourists and their stacks of luggage plus the extra influx of day-trippers from the hotel zone in Cancun.

"You booked a taxi, right?" She asked for the sixth or seventh time. "Yasmin asked if we wanted a ride to the ferry but I said, no, it wasn't necessary, because you had already arranged for taxi to pick us up."

"I did, but we don't need one," Mike said, setting his phone on the table. "We aren't going to California."

"We aren't going to California?" Jessica repeated, nearly shouting. "Why not?"

"My contract has been delayed a few months, or perhaps indefinitely. Apparently, the virus has everyone worried."

Jessica slumped onto a chair. "But we have plane tickets," she moaned. "I've quit my job and given Yasmin my golf cart. Sparky has his travel papers. We have to go, Mike."

"But you didn't give up your casa yet, so we can stay here while we figure this out," Mike replied. "It's just a bump in the road, Jess, a *tope*," he said meaning a speedbump.

"I don't know your financial situation, Mike, but I need to work to feed myself and my dog," she said. "I'll call Carlos and beg him to take me back at *Loco Lobo*."

"Or we could all go on doggie rations?"

"Have you seen what I cook for Sparky?" Jessica lifted one blond eyebrow. "It's not cheap."

"Yes, I know," Mike acknowledged. "In the meantime, let's get to work and cancel what we can. You deal with the taxi and the airport shuttle service. I'll try to get through to the airlines," he said, rolling his eyes at the improbability of connecting with a person in customer service before their scheduled flight time.

Corked

At the Ultramar ferry dock, a substantial figure in a fuzzy red costume stood at the front of a cluster of people who appeared to be waiting, for something or someone.

The man turned to the woman beside him and mumbled a question through the mouth of the Elmo costume: "Do you see them yet? Jessica told me they would be catching the noon boat."

"No, no sign of them yet." Cristina Avalos Velazquez tipped a smile at her husband. He was wearing a full-body, and very hot, costume borrowed from their friend Freddy Medina.

Diego reached up and pulled the large fur-covered, foam head off. "God, this thing is hot!"

"You're the doofus who wanted to wear it," Cristina retorted.

"*Papi*, you are not supposed to take your head off in public!" His youngest daughter, Ana, protested. "*Tio* Freddy said so."

"I know sweetie, but *papi* is very, very hot and uncomfortable," he explained, and then upended the bottle of cool water that Cristina had handed him.

"Tio Freddy said you'll make the little kids cry if they see Elmo remove his head." Ana wasn't about to give up easily.

"Yes, I know, Diego said as he bent over to speak directly to Ana, "but other than you, there are no little kids here right now. And I didn't make you cry. Right?"

"No, that's because I'm *muy adulto*, grown-up. That's what *mami* said. I don't cry like the little kids do."

"*Si,* Ana, you are *muy adulto*," Diego agreed, stifling a smile as he hugged his four-year-old daughter, then he turned his attention to Cristina. "I just wanted to give Jess something to smile about. She's pretty emotional about leaving the island," he said, "but I am going to die of heat exhaustion if she doesn't get here soon."

"I'll call her," Cristina offered, tapping the buttons on her cell phone. Diego opened his mouth to add something more, but she held up her forefinger and thumb in the familiar *wait a minute* gesture. "*Hola Jess, ¿Cómo está?*"

"*Bien, bien, ¿et tu?*" Jessica answered.

"*Todo bien, gracias.* What boat are you catching?"

"Oh god, Cristina! We've had a sudden change of plans," Jessica's voice boomed through the tiny speaker, "We aren't leaving today. Mike's contract has been cancelled, or delayed, or something."

Cristina's gaze swept over the large gathering of friends waiting on the dock for the departure of Jessica, Sparky, and Mike. Many held colorful signs with various expressions of well wishes, and happy new adventures. Turning to look at Diego, Cristina spoke loudly so that the others would hear, "Not leaving today? I'm sad for you, but happy for us," she replied holding one hand up in a what-the-hell gesture.

"Cristina, I'm so sorry. Mike and I are scrambling to cancel our travel plans. Can we call you back later?" Jessica replied.

"*Si*, of course. We'll chat later," she said disconnecting the call. "Did everyone hear that? Jessica and Mike aren't leaving—just yet. They've had an unexpected change in their plans."

Amid moans of disappointment for their aborted send-off celebration, but expressions of happiness that their friends were staying, the crowd slowly disbanded, heading back to their various vehicles.

"I want my going-away gift back," grumbled Diego.

Cristina tipped her face up, her brown eyes studied his, "You didn't buy her anything. You told me that wearing this silly costume was her gift."

Two hours later, Mike picked up a pen and drew a neat line. "One more thing completed," he said. "How are you doing on your list?"

"I cancelled the taxi and contacted the airport shuttle service. They didn't give us a refund but did issue credit to use when we do leave," Jessica said, reading from her notes, "and I told my landlord we would be staying a bit longer. He's fine with that. I'd already arranged to keep the house for a few months anyway." She stretched, placed both hands on Mike's shoulders and dug her fingers into his tight muscles. "How about you?"

"Ah, that feels so good," he said, relaxing into the massage. "I finally got through to the airline, and was able to change our tickets. They did the same thing — gave us a credit to use when we figure out our departure dates, but it is only good for one year."

"Surely we'll be gone by then!"

"Who knows what's going to happen." Mike was staring thoughtfully at Sparky. "Jess, I'm going to do everything I can to get another contract, but I should warn you, we might have a small problem," he said, nodding toward the dog. "The little guy can only come with us if my next contract is the U.S. or Canada."

"I know," she gave his back a final rub, then sat down, "Any other country and he'd have to go into quarantine for up to six months, and I can't do that to him.".

"I understand." Mike nodded. "So, in that case you'd stay here on Isla?"

"That's the easiest solution," she said. Mike's eyes dimmed a little when she confirmed that without Sparky, she wouldn't go with him. "I already have this house and I'm pretty sure I can get my job back at *Loco Lobo*, but everything depends on what happens with your work."

"Okay, let's deal with one problem at a time," he said reaching for her hand. "But, right now, let's order in, open a bottle of wine, and wind down a bit. My brain is overloaded and I need to decompress."

"Sure, but I have one more phone call to make. I have to explain to Yasmin that we need to take *Frida Bandita* back for a bit, and to beg for a job."

"About that comment you made a few days ago," Mike said.

"What comment?"

"Coronavirus: It's not my problem." His lips tweaked in a half-smile.

"All right, I admit it. I have my head in the sand when it comes to world events." She heard

Corked

Mike's sputter of laughter as she picked up her phone.

Chapter 5

Isla Mujeres

Mike opened his Google contacts and scanned the list. *Who's my best bet to find out what was happening in the industry? Eric? He's a competitor for work, but he's a good guy.* Mike swiped the screen on his phone and tapped in the numbers. "Hey bud, this is Mike Lyons. How're you doing?"

"Mike. What a surprise. I'm doing good," Eric answered. "What's happening with you?"

"Well, that's why I'm calling. I am looking for work," Mike said. "You know of anything?"

"Off the top of my head, no nothing. When are you available?"

Mike glanced over at the still-packed luggage. "As it turns out, immediately. I had a contract in southern California, but it was unexpectedly canceled just as we were about to head to the airport."

Corked

"I'm sorry to hear that, but I think we have a bit of catching up to do. Who is the we?" Eric asked. "And, where are you?"

"I'm in Mexico on an island called Isla Mujeres, with a woman named Jessica Sanderson. She's coming with me."

"The island of women; I've been there," Eric said. "How did you end up on Isla?"

"A vacation last summer that stretched into several months."

"Before or after you met the lady?"

"After," Mike admitted.

"Uh huh, I figured," Eric said. "As I said, I don't know of anything off the top of my head, but give me a couple of hours to think. Is this the best number to call you back?"

"Yes, or you can pop me an email," he said. "Do you still have my email address?"

"Let's see." Mike could hear Eric tapping a few keys, then he repeated a string of letters and symbols. "It that the current one?"

"Yep, that's the one."

"Okay, I'll get back to you soon."

"Appreciate that Eric, thanks."

"Beers are on you, next time," Eric said. "Catch you later."

34

"You bet," Mike said disconnecting the call.

"Any luck?" Jessica asked. She flipped her long blond plait over one shoulder, stuffed her feet into her sandals, then picked up the keys to the golf cart.

"A friend in the industry is going to ask around. In the meantime, I have a whacking great bunch of emails to send out to my contacts at various wineries," he said. "What are you up to?"

"I'm taking Sparky for a ride and a quick dip in the ocean."

"Swimming, that sounds inviting. I wish I could join you," Mike said.

"Not me, just Sparky," she said as she clipped the leash to his harness, "I'm headed to *Loco Lobo* afterwards to talk to Carlos. He's happy to have me back, and I have to check to see when I am working. I need to top up my bank account in case we're here for a bit."

"Jess, I'm so sorry. I'll get this straightened out."

"We'll work it out, Mike. Don't worry."

"Thank you." He ran his lips over hers. "See you when you get back."

Corked

Mike stood at the window, watching Jessica pull away from the curb. Damn it. He had to find work in Canada or the United States. He wasn't going to lose her by leaving her behind while he rambled around the world supervising winemakers. Every time he looked at her, his heart squeezed with emotion. He'd never felt this way about any woman.

Pouring another cup of coffee, he sat down at his laptop. He planned to send a letter of inquiry to a selection of the eight hundred Canadian wineries and the eleven thousand American operations. He'd stick with the small to medium sized companies, because many of the larger ones had university educated vintners and they didn't need his expertise.

He sighed. It really was just busy work until he heard back from Eric, but at the same time he couldn't just hang around and hope that his friend could find him a lead. Diligence was the key to finding another contract.

Fifteen minutes later, Jessica stopped her golf cart at a neighborhood playground on the eastern side of the island. It had public access to the ocean and it was one of Sparky's favorite swimming holes. The tiny beach was stuck in between two truck-sized chunks of compressed sand that had broken off the island in the last storm. Either one of the pieces could have crushed both Sparky and her if they had been nearby when it happened. She had visions of being squashed under the enormous chunks like the wicked witch in the Wizard of Oz, with just her legs visible for the world to know of her demise.

"Come on, pooch, let's get you cooled down," she said, unclipping his leash which was wound around the back seat as a makeshift doggie seatbelt. He ran to the beach, dashed chest-deep into the turquoise water and stopped with his feet still on solid ground. "Silly boy, you love the ocean, but you're not fond of swimming," she said as she followed him, wading deeper until it lapped at the hem of her shorts. The temperature was perfect.

Bored, Sparky left the water and began to hunt the tiny white sand crabs that lived along the edge of the water. He dug energetically, hoping to catch one unaware, but Jessica could see the little creatures scuttle away from his frenzied excavations. Keeping an eye on him, she examined the fallen masses. Remembering some of the basic geology her grandfather had taught her, she mused over the formation of the island.

Isla was essentially a large sandbar that had over the centuries poked out of the ocean to create a palm tree clad piece of paradise. The highest elevation was twenty-three meters, or about seventy-five feet, above sea level. Since the island was primarily made of compressed sand, it stood to reason that the ocean had, at some point, covered the island for a significantly long time.

Corked

A few weeks ago, she had been browsing the internet and discovered that the last time the sea level was higher than today was during the Eemian Period, about 130,000 years ago. That was well before man had become industrialized enough to have any impact on weather patterns.

How long ago had Isla become an island? Tens of thousands of years ago?

"Enough daydreaming," she said to herself. "Come on Sparky, we have stuff to do," Jessica said, heading up the pathway.

He followed her, and vigorously showered her with a combination of seawater and sand just before hopping back into the cart.

Chapter 6

No Regrets Winery

Occupied with reading the contents of an unlabeled file folder, Ellen Taylor bumped the filing drawer closed with her hip. Her head bent over the pages and concentrating on the information, she didn't hear the footsteps.

"Hey Ellen."

She flinched, snapped the file shut then dropped it to her side. "Ben, you startled me. I didn't hear you." She felt the telltale flush of heat creep up her neck, and prayed he wouldn't notice her discomfort.

Ben Whitaker let his eyes fall to the folder. "Are you reading something interesting?"

"No, no. Just the monthly sales. I'm working on the tedious LDB reports," she stammered. It was a plausible explanation. The BC Liquor Distribution Branch was the governing body for any company producing, distributing, or selling any type of alcoholic beverages and the monthly reports were time-consuming. "Can I do something for you, Ben?"

"I just shipped a pallet of Pinot Blanc to the Vancouver warehouse," he said, tossing the papers on her desk. He gave her a look that was an unclear mix of defiance and pride.

Puzzled, Ellen asked, "When did we get Pinot Blanc?"

"Wine magic," he smirked, "wine magic, baby."

"Ben. What did you do?"

"Chardonnay. Pinot Blanc," he tipped his hand back and forth. "You have to be an expert to tell them apart, especially when the Chard is unoaked."

"Please tell me you didn't." She couldn't believe what she was hearing.

"The boss knows all about it." He flipped his hand in the general direction of Quartermain's empty office. "Our new sales rep doesn't know his ass from a hole in the ground. He sold a product that we don't make, but the boss didn't want to blow the sale. He told me to bottle a pallet of Pinot Blanc," Ben's face twisted in a cocky smirk. "So, I did."

Ellen watched him do that annoying air quote thing, and she stifled the urge to smack him with the file folder, the one that she didn't want anyone to know about. "If the BCLDB finds out we will be in big trouble."

"Just chill; no one will know," he said.

"But how could you label a wine we don't make?"

"I don't know where or how the boss got the labels, but he did." He turned and sauntered toward the door, lifting one hand in a nonchalant wave. "I'm off the clock. Catch you tomorrow."

"Damn it!" Ellen sputtered, to his back. She chewed the inside of her cheek, thinking it's just one more illegal thing that Quartermain was doing. She still hadn't heard from Daniel Cooper about when, or if, the accountants were going to do a full audit. She was beginning to doubt her decision to confide in him.

Maybe Daniel had told Quartermain that she knew he was fleecing the shareholders. And maybe Quartermain had made a deal with Daniel Cooper to falsify the audit and now he was looking for a plausible reason to fire her. Why hadn't she minded her own business? Kept her head down and ignored his theft? She sighed. She was certain Quartermain had purposely involved her in his scam so that he would have someone to deflect the blame to when the shit hits the fan.

She opened the folder in her hand and reread the documents. It was still the same damning information as the last time she had read it. Quartermain had funneled a large amount of the investors cash into purchasing a separate acreage, large enough to build another winery.

His name was on the title. Not the company's name. Just his.

Should she call Daniel with this additional information? Moving to the photocopier she removed the staple, placed the documents in the slot, pushed start and watched as the machine pulled each page into its maw, and then spewed out the original and a copy. She stapled the originals and filed them back in the drawer, keeping the copies for herself. *Now what?*

She hunted through the boxes of stationery looking for a plain envelope, one without the company logo and return address. She folded the pages to fit the envelope and was about to lick the glue to seal the flap, but paused. Holding the packet in her hands a wave of paranoia made her hands tremble. Her DNA in the saliva, her fingerprints on the paper. *Would it come to that?*

Ellen hurried to where her coat was hanging and searched for her gloves. She pulled them on, removed the paper from the envelope and scrubbed a tissue over everything hoping to at least smear her fingerprints. She refolded the papers and stuffed them inside the packet, then moistened the tissue in the glass of water sitting on her desk, and used it to wet the glue. In childish block printing she added on the front, "Daniel

Cooper Private and Confidential," then sealed the envelope and shoved it deep into her leather purse.

Checking the time, she turned off the lights and locked the door to the office. It was late and the building was deadly quiet. Everyone but good old reliable Ellen had left for the day.

She unlocked her hatchback, started the engine, and let it idle while the heater gusted barely warm air on the ice-covered windshield. The sun had set two hours ago, and the stars were brilliant white shapes in the dark winter sky. The polar vortex was slowly receding and as it moved back north the temperatures were warming to a bearable level.

Tilting her head close to the driver's window she studied the sky. The moon was a thin waning crescent while the seven bright stars in the Orion constellation stood tall a little to the south. The planet Neptune was visible with the naked eye, and the Ursa Major, the Big Dipper was easy to locate. One day, she promised herself, she would spend a restful weekend stargazing on Anarchist Mountain near Osoyoos. There were two guest houses that had privately owned observatories. Both were perfect locations for quietly sipping good wine and gazing at the glorious array of heavenly bodies and faraway galaxies.

With a bump, her wandering imagination landed back in her frigid car. There wouldn't be any relaxing getaways until this mess was sorted out at

Corked

the winery. She turned on the wipers, clearing away the melted frost, and put the transmission in gear.

Driving north into the larger city of Penticton, she parked outside an impressive office building and studied the entry. Just as she had hoped, there was a mail slot in the glass door. She scurried toward the entrance and using her gloved hands, tipped her delivery through the slot.

Daniel might believe she was the source of this new information, but he couldn't easily prove it.

Chapter 7

Isla Mujeres

"*Madre de Dios*, Jessica, why are you back working at *Loco Lobo*?" Filipe Ramirez pulled out a chair and sat at a table in her section. "I thought you had moved to California with that *gringo* guy, Mike Lyons."

"*Hola* Filipe," she greeted the municipal police sergeant, "I just couldn't leave you," she patted him lightly on the shoulder and placed a menu in front of him. "I assume you're hungry?" She hadn't seen him since the murder of Brandon Forbes, and she tamped down her irritation at his insensitive remark that she was in some way responsible for the increase in suspicious deaths on the island.

"You couldn't leave me?" He tipped his head so that he could make eye contact, and asked, "What does that mean?"

"If I left the island you wouldn't have anything to do. You'd be bored silly." She noticed his uniform fit snuggly over his wide chest, and the dark blue material accented his black hair and deep brown eyes. He was a decent looking guy, with a nice smile, but Filipe had a reputation for roving eyes, and hands.

"Bored! Ha, I might actually have time for something other than cleaning up your messes," he declared.

"Now, now, don't be mean," she said, with a dry laugh. "Is Alexis joining you for lunch?" She placed a second menu on the table.

"Uh, no," Filipe glanced down. "She's not." His voice was flat.

"Isn't she working today?" Jessica asked, and picked up the unnecessary menu. Filipe and Alexis were partners at work and at home. She rarely saw one without the other.

"I don't know," He flicked his eyes up, and then back to the table. "She left me, moved to Cancun, and now she's a constable with the *Policía Estatal*."

"I'm sorry to hear that you aren't together anymore, but good for her landing another policing position." Jessica noticed his bewildered expression and could guess what was coming next.

"I don't understand why she left me," he protested. "Sure, I cheated on her a few times, but it wasn't serious."

Jessica stared at him, wondering if he really was as dense as he sounded.

"And," he continued, oblivious to her glare, "most of the time I kept it in the family. I mainly fooled around with her younger sister."

"Her sister?" She hadn't been expecting that response. She was certain he'd had numerous affairs because she had seen him in action, seducing other women, but the doing the horizontal tango with the younger sister—that was a shock.

"It's no big deal," he replied.

Incredulous, Jessica bit back her response. "Can I get you a drink while you decide on what you want to eat?" she asked, keeping a smile on her lips. Until this moment Filipe had been a friend, not as close as Diego or Carlos but still someone she had begun to rely on. He had, after all, been the one who had shot and killed her assailant the previous year, but right now, she wanted tell him he was an inconsiderate *pendjo* and that she was happy that Alexis had dumped him.

"*Si, una Sol. Gracias.*"

Five minutes later she returned and set the beer in front of him. "*De nada.* Have you decided on what you want yet?"

He sighed, closed the menu and took a long pull of his beer, but didn't answer her question.

"Do you know what you want, Filipe?" she asked again.

He turned his dark eyes on her. "Are you going to stay on the island, Jessica?"

Oh crap, he's hitting on me. "Just for a few more weeks. Mike and I have some things to sort out," she said and shifted so that she wasn't within pawing distance of his hands. Touching, hugging, and kissing friends was part of the Mexican culture, and a demeaning pat on the rump wasn't a crime, but she wasn't going to give him the opportunity to maul her.

"Well, you let me know if that doesn't work out for you," he said, giving her a long look that clearly indicated his meaning. "I could show you a really good time."

"Enjoy your beer, Filipe. I'll check back later," she said, walking away. Corruption was rampant among the Mexican *policía*. She could find herself in a difficult situation if she made a scene, and punching a police sergeant was never a wise move, in any culture.

She exhaled a long breath, and caught Yasmin's eye. "It's not too busy right now, and I need a fifteen-minute break. Can Camilla cover my section?"

"You look flushed. Are you feeling okay?" Yasmin answered.

Jessica nodded her head toward the police sergeant's broad back, "A bit of a problem. I'll explain later," she said, removing her server's apron and hanging it on a hook behind the bar.

Twenty minutes later Jessica returned to *Loco Lobo* and retrieved her apron. She glanced over at the table where Ramirez had been sitting. "When did Filipe leave?" She asked.

"As soon as Camilla asked him for his order. He slammed some money on the table to pay for his beer and left," Yasmin said. "What's that all about?"

Jessica made a face. "He hit on me and I brushed him off."

"That's just Filipe, Jess; he's horny and hits on every female," Yasmin said, "He'd probably proposition my mother and my grandmother."

"I agree," Jessica said, "and I'd pay to watch your formidable mother and grandmother cut him down to size, but this time it was different. Alexis dumped him, and his ego is fragile."

"Alexis Gomez dumped him? That must be difficult since they work together and he's her boss," Yasmin said.

"She got another job with the state police, and moved to Cancun."

Corked

"Good for her," Yasmin agreed. "That explains why he's sulking. In all the years that I have known Filipe, nobody, and I mean nobody, has ever dumped him."

"Well, hopefully I can avoid him until we leave the island." Jessica motioned to Camilla that she was back working her section. "Let's talk about something else. Any special plans to celebrate your anniversary on Saturday?"

"Dinner out, maybe. This is high season, Carnaval starts tonight, and all the good restaurants will be jammed," Yasmin sighed. "Being restaurateurs, you would think we could have chosen a quieter time to be married, but no, we picked the Saturday closest to my birthday and the busiest time of the year."

"You're right, not good planning," Jessica agreed.

"We also talked about a two-week getaway, but decided against it because of the construction costs of our new, but un-named restaurant."

"You still hadn't decided on a name?"

"It's all your fault," Yasmin pointed an accusing finger at Jessica.

Jessica laid the palm of her hand on her breast bone and innocently asked, "My fault?"

"Yes, yours," Yasmin said, "Carlos and Diego are obsessed with your suggestion of *A Pirate's Delight*."

"What's wrong with the name?" Jessica asked, with a cheeky grin.

"It was perfect until you told us about the double meaning. About how your grandfather referred to a woman with a flat chest as a sunken treasure or a pirate's delight," Yasmin said, her lips curled up in a smirk. "I don't like the off-color connotation, but I have to admit the name is a perfect fit for a pirate-themed eatery."

"Then go with it, have a bit of fun."

Chapter 8

Isla Mujeres

"Hallelujah!" Mike shouted, as he reread the email in his inbox.

"Good news?" Jessica asked. She hung up the dish towel she had used when cleaning up after their basic, but nutritious, lunch. One day, she resolved, she would learn to enjoy cooking. Maybe. She folded her arms and leaned back against the kitchen counter.

"I have a signed contract, starting Monday March 16th."

"That's fantastic, Mike, whereabouts?"

"At *No Regrets Winery*, in the Okanagan Valley."

"Okanagan British Columbia? Or Okanogan Washington?"

He turned in his chair and flashed a wide smile, that kind that never failed to increase her pulse rate, "BC, back in your old stomping grounds."

"Awesome, my family will be delighted." She stooped to give him a kiss just as he stood up, and banged the top of his skull against the end of her nose.

"Shit!" They said in unison. Mike rubbed the skin on top of his head. Jessica gingerly touched her nose. "Damn, that hurt. Am I bleeding?" she asked.

"Let me see." Mike removed her hand and examined her face. "No blood. A few tears in your eyes though," he said. "Let me kiss it better." He angled toward her for a gentle smooch.

"If this turns into a black eye, I am going to tell everyone that it's your fault," she mumbled under his kiss.

He unstuck his lips. "Just don't tell your cop boyfriend, Filipe, that I smacked you. He packs a really big gun."

"He's not my damn boyfriend," she objected hotly. "I shouldn't have said anything about him hitting on me."

"I'm just teasing you, babe," Mike wrapped his arms around Jessica, and smiled into her eyes, "I'm the luckiest guy alive because you are with me."

"Don't you forget it, buster." Jessica kissed him again. "Now, tell me about this winery."

"It's a bit south of Penticton, in the Okanagan Falls area. Medium-sized. And it recently changed ownership," Mike touched his lips with his thumb and forefinger, then held them up to the light. "Dog hair. Have you been necking with Sparky again?" he asked.

"Yes," she quipped. "Are you jealous?"

"A bit." He turned on the kitchen tap and stuck his fingers under the water to rinse away the strand of hair.

"Was *No Regrets* bought out by one of the big conglomerates like Arterra?" she asked.

"No, not this one," Mike said. "How do you know about Arterra?" He sat at the table, and stretched his legs out.

"I'm a B.C. girl born and bred, and I like wine and trivia sticks in my head," she said. "Constellation Brands Canada was purchased by the Ontario Teachers Pension Fund in 2016. The name was changed to Arterra Wines Canada."

Mike nodded, "Arterra owns about a dozen wineries in Canada, the US, and Australia. They aren't trivial."

"Nope, they're definitely one of the bigger players in the industry."

"Anyway, the website says the original owner was a very upbeat, positive guy. The name of his company reflected his outlook on life: no regrets, no bad memories. He recently decided to retire, and the winery has been purchased by a consortium of mostly Canadian investors."

Jessica checked the time on her phone. "Oops, it's getting late and I've got to get ready for my afternoon shift. Could you take Sparky out for a walk?"

"Does he actually walk? I thought he insisted on being chauffeured to his favorite swimming holes."

"He walks!" Jessica retorted. "Just take him for an amble around the neighborhood. It's cool enough he should be okay for twenty minutes or so."

"I've been meaning to ask, why does he get overheated so easily? He was born here on Isla."

"The dog-doc, Delfino, says Sparky has an enlarged heart and we shouldn't push him with excessive exercise. Let him set the pace. Sniff, pee, walk, sniff, pee, and walk. Rinse and repeat."

"Yes ma'am." Mike snapped off a salute.

Jessica shook her head. "You're such a goof."

"Yes ma'am. I truly am, ma'am."

"Don't forget, I will be late tonight. It's the big dance night of Carnaval and the restaurant will be packed."

Corked

Jessica jockeyed her red golf cart, *Frita Bandita*, into a miniscule parking spot a block away from *Loco Lobo*. Centro reverberated with the beat of a sexy salsa as a troop of dancers set up at the intersection of Juarez and Matamoros.

Crammed into the back of a pickup truck, a second troupe hollered greetings and squeezed past before the street was totally blocked.

Feathers. Sequins. Sexy costumes with demure skin-colored leggings. Giant headdresses. Pink, orange and purple. Orange, yellow and blue. Green, red and yellow. The color. The music. The movement. It was captivating.

The scene would be repeated again and again around town, as each dance troupe displayed their routines and hustled the crowd for tips. The tips helped to offset the cost of the dancers' costumes; three, sometimes four, different costumes were needed for the five-day event.

Saturday night was always the biggest, busiest, and noisiest night of the annual celebration. The pulsing ten-piece band would start just before midnight and rock the city until dawn. No one at the northern end of the island expected to sleep tonight.

And, dammit, she had promised to work.

Corked

Her insecurity about the situation with Mike's contract had overridden her desire to grab him and immerse themselves in the craziness. Who knew, maybe this was her last opportunity to experience Carnaval in all of its wild and noisy glory? And what about Mike? She hadn't thought to ask, but maybe he had never experienced the riotous event. They had both thought they would be working in California by now, not still here on the island. Hopefully there would be another chance to enjoy the annual event together.

Even on a normal night the vibe of Centro was infectious. The streets had been laid out a few hundred years before vehicles were invented. The narrow tracks were barely wide enough for one parked car and one moving vehicle. In the evenings guitarists or groups of mariachis wandered the streets asking restaurant patrons the same question: *¿Música amigo?*

The busy souvenir stores, the lively restaurants, and hawkers of Oaxaca cheese, fresh pastries, popsicles, ice cream, and the delicious dessert marquesitas all contributed to an untidy and lively atmosphere.

For a good time come to Isla! Or maybe, for a good time call Isla. That would make a great bumper sticker, she thought to herself as she dodged through the crowd, headed toward *Loco Lobo*.

"Jessica!" Behind her a masculine voice called her name.

She turned to look, just as a woman jostled her and sent her crashing into Sergeant Filipe Ramirez.

"This is nice," Ramirez said, encircling her with his arms. "Have you been avoiding me?"

"No, Filipe, I haven't." She shook her head and disengaged from his grip. "Mike and I have been really busy. I'm working full time at *Loco Lobo*, and Mike has been searching for work," she said, deliberately repeating Mike's name.

Filipe's eyes pinned hers, oblivious to the crowd of spectators jostling their way past on the narrow sidewalk. "Did he find a job?"

"Yes, as a matter of fact he did," she said. "We're headed to Canada, soon. Very soon." She emphasised, without revealing their intended departure date.

"Remember what I said," he leaned closer and she could feel his hot breath on her cheek, as his finger traced the length of her forearm. "I'd be happy to show you a good time — anytime. And I won't mind if you have your *gringo* boyfriend on the side."

Suppressing the urge to wipe where his hand had touched her, she flashed an insincere smile and said, "I've gotta go to work. I hope you don't have too much trouble with the Carnaval celebrations."

She slipped into the throng. *Take the hint, and leave me alone.*

Chapter 9

Isla Mujeres

Jessica surveyed her little *casa* and sighed. It was a colorful nest, a combination of navy, pink, orange, and turquoise. She knew at some point she would have to sell or give away her furniture and cancel her lease agreement with her landlord, but for now, she wanted to keep things as they were. This was her fallback position, in case things didn't work out in Canada with Mike's employment, or for that matter between Mike and her.

She loved him, but they were still new to this relationship and anything could happen.

"Hey beautiful, are you daydreaming?" Mike asked.

Jessica nodded her head. "Yep, I was. What did I miss?" She asked. He was standing in front of the refrigerator with the door open, and an expectant look on his face.

"I'm cleaning the fridge. Anything I should keep this time around, or just toss it all out — again?"

"It's mostly condiments and the remains of take-out, so yeah, toss everything but the milk for our morning coffee, the yogurt, and Sparky's food," she said. "We can eat out tonight."

"I assumed we would go out," he agreed. "You sure we shouldn't give this to someone else?" He asked, holding up an almost new bottle of mayonnaise.

"No," Jessica motioned with her hands. "You have no idea how many of my friends give me their leftovers when they are closing up their homes for the summer. One year I ended up with a bunch of mustards, five ketchups, and four bottles of mayo. I don't want to pass along my condiments to other friends."

"Your wish is my command, *Princesa*," he said, with a mock bow and dropped it, plus a handful of open bottle and containers, into the garbage can sitting at his feet. "Where do you want to go for dinner?"

Jessica thought for a minute, "I'm torn. *Loco Lobo* to say goodbye to everyone again, or *Bally Hoo* to watch the sunset, or *Rosa Sirena's* so we can say goodbye to Deb and Willy," With indecision reflected in her expression, she asked, "What do you want to do?"

"Sunset at *Bally Hoo*. Since we are headed to the Far Frozen North this will be our last tropical sunset for awhile."

"Good choice."

He opened the freezer. "Nothing but ice cubes in here," he said emptying the trays into the sink. "Are we unplugging the fridge tomorrow morning?"

"Nope, the landlord says it's better for it to keep working." Jessica's lips tweaked up, as she watched him work. "It's a good thing you can cook or you might starve to death waiting for me to create something edible out of ice cubes and condiments."

"I've been single a long time. I've learned to fend for myself." He closed the freezer door and replaced the garbage can under the sink. "I'll empty that later and put the big can on the street when we are all done cleaning up."

Jessica put her arms around him. "You don't talk about her much."

"Lisa? Umm," he said, "not much to say. We married young, grew apart, and divorced years ago." His eyes held a hint of sadness.

"Do you ever hear from her?"

"No." Mike shook his head. "No children and no reason to keep in touch. She's remarried and I've been told she has a boy and a girl." He bent his head and rested his forehead against hers. "How about you? Any near misses with marriage?"

"One, but I decided I wanted to travel instead of settling down."

"And he didn't?"

"Nope, strictly white picket fence and two-point-four kids, a mortgage, and absolutely no desire to travel."

"Lucky for me." Mike's lips brushed hers, then the kiss became more intense as she fumbled to unzip his shorts. "I think we should get a room," he murmured. "We wouldn't want to embarrass Sparky."

"Damn, I'm going to miss this," Jessica said, tilting her face toward the streaks of orange, purple, pink, and crimson coloring the sky. "This is one of my favorite places on the island. The boats coming and going, the long stretch of sand, families swimming, lovers enjoying the sunset. It's perfect."

"It is beautiful. I'll miss it too," Mike agreed. He reached under the table and scratched the top of Sparky's head. "How about you mutt-ski, are you going to miss your island?"

Jessica turned her attention from the sunset and beamed at him. "And now you are having heart-to-heart talks with my dog."

Mike straightened up. "He's a good listener." He tipped his beer and sucked in a swallow.

"And I'm not?"

"Sometimes you're not."

"Really, and when exactly would that be?"

"This morning, when I read you an article about COVID-19 being declared a worldwide pandemic."

"And," she pulled a face and rolled her hand in a give-me-more motion.

"Your response was 'uh huh'."

"What did you expect me to say?"

"I don't know," Mike admitted. "How about something like, oh shit, we should have kept the condiments and stayed on Isla."

Jessica put her glass of Malbec on the table, and leveled her sapphire blue eyes at Mike. "Do you genuinely believe that's what we should do?"

He crooked his arm, propping his chin in one hand and said, "Honestly, Jess, I don't have a clue. I have a signed contract but as we both know that doesn't mean a damn thing in these circumstances. A month ago, I had a contract with a different winery that was canceled at the last minute. The worldwide situation is changing daily." He unzipped the beer cozy, turned to look for their waiter, and held the empty bottle aloft.

Across the room the waiter nodded, then pointed at Jessica.

"Do you want another, Jess?"

"No, I'm good for now."

Mike made eye contact again with the waiter and shook his head, then he reached out and took Jessica's hand. "The other thing that is nagging at me is an email that I received from the Canadian government yesterday."

"That sounds ominous. Are we going to be arrested when we land?"

"No." Bemused, he shook his head. He knew by her expression she was joking about the arrest comment, but he really was concerned about the email. "However, the message advised me to return to Canada as soon as possible because there is a possibility all the flights will be canceled and we won't be able to return."

"I know," Jessica nodded, "I'm registered with the passport office too, and I got the same email. I didn't say anything about it because I knew we were headed back tomorrow," she said with a sigh. "But you know, a part of me asks, what the hell would be wrong with not being able to leave this piece of paradise for a long, long time."

Corked

"I know what you mean," Mike took the fresh beer from the waiter's hand. "Gracias, Miguel," he said and slipped it into the beer cozy.

"It's an adventure, Mike. Let's toast our future, whatever it may be," Jessica lifted her drink.

"You're right; it is an adventure." He clinked his bottle against the rim of her glass. "To our unpredictable and crazy future!"

"That's the best kind."

Corked

Chapter 10

No Regrets Winery

Ellen Taylor surveyed the roomy but chilly barrel room. Sturdy metal racks were stacked floor to ceiling with expensive French oak barrels. The barrels cradled red wines from previous vintages, slumbering into a mellow maturity before being bottled. The room had an earthy odor of crushed fruit, mold, and yeast. Spring decorations, crisp white linens, polished cutlery and an array of five glasses at each place setting changed the serviceable work space into convivial setting for a gourmet multi-course dinner.

Outside, an unseasonably late and heavy snow drifted down. If the guests hadn't heeded her previous email advising them to dress warmly, she had a stack of microfiber throws ready to be handed out, similar to the business-class blankets on an airline. In a predictable display of extravagance, Kingsley had ordered fifty of the dark blue, lap-sized throws embroidered with the corporate logo. He intended to give a blanket to each person as their personal memento of the evening. The cost per item was in excess of their

67

most expensive bottle, and she was certain the shareholders would have enjoyed the wine as much, if not more, than a piece of cloth.

"Ellen," Kingsley said, catching her attention.

"Yes?"

"All set?"

"Yes, everything is ready." She was dreading this evening. She had hoped the accountants would find a way to do a forensic audit before this meeting, but it seemed to be a faint hope. She knew Kingsley's after-dinner speech was focused on how well the company was doing according to his inflated sales figures. His brazen overselling of the shares would not be mentioned, but sooner or later someone would find out. "Should I escort the guests in?"

"Yup. Let's get the dog and pony show on the road." He winked at her.

Her guts cramped with tension. She was unhappy that he presumed she was complicit in his illegal activities. She pulled open the heavy wooden doors separating the gift shop from the warehouse. "Please," she said as she motioned the group forward, "join us. We're all set for a fabulous evening."

They ambled in, carrying glasses of a crisp and newly released sparking wine made exclusively from Chardonnay grapes. Ellen could hear snippets of their conversations. Someone was describing it as having notes of yellow apple, citrus, tropical fruits, and a touch of peach. Another couple chattered about how beautiful the winery was, and what a gorgeous venue it would be for their daughter's wedding. Ellen breathed in and closed her eyes for a brief moment to steady herself, then forced a welcoming smile onto her face. "Please take a seat anywhere you like, except the chair designated for the president," she said, sweeping a hand toward the tables.

Kingsley posed photogenically in front of the impressive oak barrels, holding a balloon glass of a dark, rich Cabernet Sauvignon in his hand. His white collared shirt, a dark blue V-neck pullover, and snug designer jeans screamed sex appeal and money. He waited until everyone was seated and looking expectantly his way, then he started his welcome speech.

"Welcome everyone to our first bi-annual shareholders celebration. Tonight, we will enjoy a taste-tingling blend of flavors. Each of the five courses will be served with one of our award-winning wines that has been chosen by our master chef and myself to complement the intriguing flavors," he said. "Our first course will be a truffle and smoked black cod custard complemented by heritage tomatoes and fresh marjoram harvested from our own herb garden. It will be paired with our premium Chardonnay. Enjoy!"

Corked

On cue, the wait staff began to place the artistically presented appetizer in front of each guest. The conversation level rose, ricocheting off of the hard surfaces of the barrel room.

Satisfied that the event was off to a good start, Quartermain sat at his place and picked up a fork. Judging by the animated expressions and voluble conversations, the investors appeared to be relishing the experience. In his view it was all about appearances, the perception, the bragging rights, and having a decent drinkable product: wines that could on occasion win a 'Best of' in competition. Many of the newer wineries were not profitable, relying on cash calls to shareholders for operating funds. Some of the industry insiders liked to joke, "How do you make a small fortune in a winery? Start with a large fortune."

The evening continued with two more dishes and finally the main course of delectable Saltspring Island lamb chops, served with tiny roasted beets, baby carrots, and petite potatoes. Each course was accompanied by a wine especially chosen to complement the flavors. Ellen was uncomfortably stuffed. She had tried her best to only eat half of what she had been served, but in the end the delicious flavors had won out and she had cleaned her plate with every course.

When the plates for the main course were cleared away, and the delicate chocolate mousse had been offered to each guest, Kingsley stood to address the crowd. "I would like to thank the people responsible for this fabulous dinner," he said, gesturing toward the chef and sous chef who were standing in the front of the servers. He clapped loudly and appreciatively, bringing the diners to their feet in enthusiastic agreement.

"Now, please be seated and we will press on to the business portion of the evening," Kingsley said, motioning for the lights to be dimmed. Over the muted clatter of dessert spoons on dishes and a late harvest dessert wine being poured into tiny flutes, he ran through his material, pausing in a well-practiced manner to allow the audience to react to a witticism.

As the presentation finished and the lights were turned up Matthew Douglas, the chairman of the board of directors, stood up. "Congratulations, Kingsley, great job. Now could you give us a quick update of the shareholders and their share percentage?" he asked.

Ellen's head popped up. He must know. *Daniel must have finally told him about the discrepancy.* She guiltily closed her phone, hoping no one had noticed her reading her social media feeds during Kingsley's puffed-up, self-congratulating speech.

"Matthew, great idea, but unfortunately I didn't think of that before the meeting," Kingsley agreed amicably.

"Too bad," Douglas said, "I think it would be informative."

"Tomorrow. We'll get that ready. Ellen," he said, pointing at her, "prepare a statement in the morning and email each shareholder."

"No need to email everyone," Douglas said, a smile that wasn't really a smile played on his lips. "We have another gathering tomorrow afternoon to taste the barrel samples of the red wines," he said. "You could simply post the spreadsheet on the wall," he paused, then added, "... in plain view."

His emphasis of the words *in plain view* triggered a buzz of whispered questions and raised eyebrows.

Ellen willed herself to smile in agreement at Kingsley and the director. "Yes, of course. I'll do that first thing in the morning."

"Good." Douglas dipped his chin once in acknowledgement. "Now let's enjoy the rest of the evening," he said. Turning his attention to his wife, he asked, "Would you like more, darling?"

Ellen's eyes flicked briefly toward Kingsley. His expression was impassive, but his pupils had expanded, pushing his dark brown irises into thin margins encircling two black holes. She had seen that look before on a man who was about to attack another with his fists and feet. Rage. Incandescent rage.

Corked

Her hands trembled as she quickly averted her eyes.

Chapter 11

Isla Mujeres

"Here we go again." Jessica turned her head and looked at Mike. He was perched on the back seat and surrounded by luggage. "A month later and we're headed again to the ferry terminal with our suitcases and Sparky."

"Hopefully, I won't get another text canceling this contract," Mike said.

"Just don't answer your phone, Mike," Yasmin said as she wheeled Jessica's golf cart into the curved drop-off zone at the Ultramar passenger ferry and stopped. "I'll drop you here, park the cart, and then come back to say goodbye."

"*Gracias, hermanita*," Jessica stepped out and tugged lightly on Sparky's lead to get him to follow her. "Hopefully this time is the charm."

"Suitcases, lady?" asked an elderly baggage handler, *el maletero*, who along with several other men carted luggage and boxes to the boats in exchange for tips.

Corked

"*Si, gracias*," Jessica said, letting him lift the bags into his battered bicycle-cart.

Mike grabbed the laptop. "I'll hang onto this," he said.

With tickets in hand Jessica walked into the terminal, followed by Sparky and Mike. A crush of people greeted them including Carlos Mendoza plus Cristina Avalos and her four youngsters, but oddly Diego Avalos was absent. She turned to ask Cristina where Diego was, but instead found herself face-to-face with Cristina's brother, Pedro Velazquez, and his girlfriend Maricruz Zapata.

"We are going to miss you, my friend," Pedro said, giving her an affectionate but awkward hug that squashed her handbag and Sparky's leash against her chest. He released her, and Maricruz was the next in line.

"Have fun on your new adventure and stay healthy. The island won't be the same without you." Maricruz gave Jessica a kiss on the cheek.

The remaining few minutes flew by with a dizzying mix of good friends and co-workers contributing their teary-eyed hugs and affectionate kisses. Some held shabby signs recycled from their original departure date with expressions of love and friendship. Jessica had trouble seeing where she was going. Her damn eyes kept filling up with tears.

And then a red furry creature wrapped her in a fierce hug, crushing her to its chest. "I'm going to miss you, *mi hermana*," Diego's muffled voice came from inside the large, furry head.

"Diego! Where did you get the costume?" She sniffed and wiped her nose with a bit of paper towel that she had stuffed into her pocket — just in case her emotions went wild. It had been a good decision, she thought as she honked her nose.

"I borrowed it from Freddy Medina; he uses it for the annual Elmo's Christmas Caravan."

"I love it, but you're killing me," she said. "I didn't think it would be so difficult to say goodbye to everyone."

"It's only temporary," Diego stated. "You'll return to paradise. You're an honorary islander and part Mexican, now."

Jessica nodded. "Yes, we will, mi hermano, but I'm just not sure when." She could see Mike was occupied with shaking hands and saying goodbye. He had made a lot of friends on the island in the few short months that he had lived here, and she was certain he would be willing to return for visits between his contracts, but she had no idea of when that would happen.

"I know you'll come back," Diego insisted.

The Ultramar ticket-taker unhooked the rope barrier and waved the passengers forward. Inching closer to the front of the line, Jessica gave Diego a hard hug, then handed her ticket to the agent. The agent swept the ticket under an electronic reader and handed it back to her.

"*¡Hasta luego!* See you later." She threw air kisses to everyone, and walked toward the boat.

Mike followed, put his arm around her and with Sparky walking meekly between them they trundled toward the boat: The Walk of Shame, as it was facetiously named by wintering residents returning to their chilly northern communities.

Jessica turned again, and waved at her friends, blowing kisses, and wiping tears. Damn, this was so difficult. Starting a new adventure was normally exciting and exhilarating, but this was emotionally exhausting.

And Diego, in the Elmo suit. He had almost undone her.

Scrambling up to the top deck in the pet-friendly section of the boat, Jessica turned, extended both of her arms overhead and waved vigorously at the crowd, and there was Diego, standing nearby with a large sign that read 'Our island is going to miss you!' And she started crying again.

Mike put an arm around her and gave her a squeeze. "Everyone is still hanging around waiting for the boat to depart. It's like they want to be sure, really sure, that we are leaving," he joked.

"We did abort once," she sniffed. The boat eased away from the dock, spun around and headed toward Cancun. Jessica finally sat down, and found another piece of paper towel, giving her nose a loud and juicy honk. "God, that's disgusting," she said, "I'm an ugly mess when I cry."

"You're beautiful, no matter what," Mike leaned forward and thumbed a tear off of her cheek. "This could be our last view of paradise for awhile. Let's enjoy it."

Twenty minutes later at the Cancun ferry wharf another maletero collected their bags and escorted them to the parking area for the airport shuttles. Jessica and Sparky hopped inside while Mike made sure their suitcases were stacked in the back of the van, then he joined them. "First step completed; now on to the airport," he said.

"And check-in for Sparky."

"I thought he was traveling with you in the cabin?"

"Yes, but he has to have his tummy examined for recent surgery scars and his paperwork checked."

"Surgery scars?" Mike asked. "Why do the customs officials need to know if your dog has been neutered or not?"

Corked

Jessica shook her head at Mike's naïve question. "They're looking for drug stashes sewn into his intestines, not the absence of *cajones*."

"Seriously? People do that, sew drugs into pets?"

"Apparently they do."

At the Cancun airport Jessica and Sparky waited while yet another maletero gathered their bags and asked which airline they were flying with. "WestJet, but I have to check in with immigration first," she answered.

The *maletero* nodded.

"Immigration? Why?" Mike asked.

"I have my permanent resident's card, and I have to let the Mexican authorities know that I am leaving the country; otherwise it gets messy, really messy, when I return."

The process was tedious, but expected: first the immigration line, next check in at WestJet and drop their bags, then getting Sparky examined, and finally the three of them were in the security lineup.

"Remove his harness and let him walk though on his own," the security officer said.

"Okay." Jessica leaned down to undo Sparky's gear, adding it to a bin on the conveyor belt.

79

Mike was occupied with emptying his pockets, removing the laptop from its carrier bag, and adding everything to another bin.

"Walk through," the man said.

She started walking with Sparky at her heels but the security officer held up his hand. "No, the dog has to pass separately."

Jessica stopped and pointed at the archway. "Go ahead Sparks." He stubbornly sat down and fastened his eyes on hers. The security officer glared at her as the other travelers jostled to keep their spot in the line-up.

"Let me go first," Mike suggested to the TSA agent, "I'll call him once I'm through."

"Fine."

Mike walked through without incident, then he patted his knee. "Come on Sparky." Sparky turned his head to see what Mike was doing, then refocused on Jessica.

"Go to Mike," she said. Sparky finally relented and walked through the metal detector.

Chapter 12

No Regrets Winery

Ellen distractedly read emails from customers asking about this year's releases: timing, prices, varietals. Others wanted to know about upcoming events or the bistro menu. She struggled to compose coherent answers, rechecking every email twice before hitting send.

A loud and accusatory argument raged in Kingsley's office. The six company directors were infuriated at his duplicity, reducing the value of their investments by over-selling the shares. Just this morning they had learned from the auditors that the extra cash had been primarily spent on a large acreage that was only in Quartermain's name, plus additional personal expenses. These were hard-nosed businessmen who were at the very least embarrassed and angry that a congenial con man had fleeced them, and as directors of the company they were in the precarious position of being financially accountable for Kingsley's actions.

She had to admit it; she too had been taken in by his hearty laugh, his friendly smile, and his ability to charm anyone. When he had offered her the position of office manger it had seemed like an excellent opportunity to learn the business. A pleasant good-looking boss. A beautiful winery. Pretty damn perfect.

The door to Kingsley's office jerked open and the chairman stormed out, trailed by the other directors. They headed directly toward Ellen, forming a threatening wall of masculinity around her desk.

"Ellen," Douglas barked.

"Yes?" She pushed her chair back, stood, and pulled her spine straight. She wasn't going to meekly cower or take the blame for Kingsley's deceitfulness.

"Kingsley is no longer in working for us."

"All right," she said, then continued without pausing to consider their reactions, "but you do realize that, you," she motioned to indicate the half-dozen infuriated men who faced her, "you, as a group, are partly to blame for this situation?"

Outraged, a short rotund man jerked his head back as if she had slapped his face; he cursed indignantly at her. She could never remember the name of the man, just that he was abrasive and unpleasant anytime she had spoken to him.

Douglas held up his hand, signaling the others to hold their complaints. "What do you mean by that?" he demanded.

Corked

"You permitted Kingsley to have sole signing privileges for the bank accounts, with no limits on his spending or borrowing powers." Her eyes held the chairman's gaze, waiting for the explosion of self-righteous denial, but it never came.

In the silence that followed, the men exchanged awkward glances, then Douglas quietly agreed. "You're right. We didn't keep tabs on him. We would like you to manage the winery and bistro until we hire a replacement general manager."

"All right. Which one of you will be my contact person for major decisions?" Ellen asked.

"I'll be," Douglas said, handing her his business card with his contact information. "I've written my private cell number and my home phone on the back. We'll sort out the details tomorrow." Then as a unit the men turned and stomped out the door.

Stunned, Ellen shifted her gaze from their retreating backs to Kingsley's office. Leaning casually against the door frame he stared at her, his head cocked to one side like a cat examining a cornered mouse.

Fear crawled down her spine. The directors had left their disgraced, and now unemployed, general manager still in the building. With her. The whistleblower. His temporary replacement. *What were they thinking? Or, not thinking*.

Corked

Moving casually toward her desk, Kingsley pulled out a chair and sat down. He crossed his legs, and regarded her. "What do the directors want me to do, Ellen?" He asked in a petulant tone. His expression reminded her of a young boy who knew exactly how to manipulate his parents to get what he wanted.

Ellen leaned against the filing cabinets and folded her arms over her chest, striving for a competent, in-charge expression. The chillingly accurate definition of a sociopath came to mind as she regarded the man. He liked to play mind games to control friends, family, co-workers, and definitely the investors. He was charismatic and charming. And clearly, he had broken numerous rules and made criminal decisions without feeling guilty for the harm he caused. Witness his earlier comments about the investors being sheep.

"They fired you, Kingsley. They want you to leave," she said. *And why didn't the cowards make you leave?*

"I don't understand what I did wrong," he said.

She drew in a breath, then asked a question that was preying on her mind, "Do you still have your keys?" *Please, please say the directors took your keys*, she whispered in her head.

He patted his pocket and smirked slyly at her. "Yes, I do. They didn't ask for them back."

84

"May I have them, please?" Concentrating on keeping her hand steady she extended it, waiting for Kingsley to drop the keys into her palm.

"No," he shook his head. "I have a few things I want to finish before I leave."

Ellen did a slow blink, and made a decision. She lowered her hand. Her safety was more important. "Okay, then, I guess you can lock up one more time. I'm headed home." If she still had a job in the morning, the first order of business was to get every lock changed. If she still had a job — after leaving him in the building on his own.

"If you're sure." Smirking, he left the question hanging in the air.

"Best of luck, Kingsley," she turned off her computer, happy that she had changed the password access just today, then she gathered up her things. "Goodnight."

"Goodnight." He whistled a few dry notes as she concentrated on walking to the door. "Sleep well," he shouted after her, "bitch."

Stepping outside, Ellen dashed through the dark snow-covered parking lot and scrambled into her Mazda, locking all the doors as soon as her legs were inside the vehicle. She started the engine, and without waiting for the defrosters to clear her windshield she backed out of the parking stall and drove away. A mile down the road, she pulled into a side road and left the engine running while she phoned the chairman, Matthew Douglas.

"Yes," he answered.

"Good evening Mr. Douglas, this is Ellen,"

"Good evening, Ellen, how can I help you?" His voice has a slight slur, perhaps he had had a cocktail or two while reviewing the financial shambles created by Kingsley.

"I don't know if you realize it, but you and the directors left without retrieving Kingsley's keys."

"Damnit!" He barked. "Did you get them back?"

"No, Kingsley was not in a mood to hand them over to me. I told him to lock up and I left about five minutes ago." The line went silent, "Mr. Douglas, are you still there?" She asked.

"Yes, I'm here. Just leave it as is, but get the locks changed tomorrow."

"It's already on my list of things to do as soon as the locksmith opens in the morning," Ellen said.

"Fine."

Ellen stared at her phone. Douglas had ended the call.

Chapter 13

No Regrets Winery

"Why? Why did you do it?" the man demanded. "Tell me!"

Quartermain ignored the man and reached for the third bottle of expensive sparkling wine that he had liberated from the tasting room. On some level he knew he shouldn't stay here and get shit-faced drunk, but to hell with them. He had the vision. He had organized the purchase from the original mister-nice-guy owner. He had made the winery an up-and-coming player in the industry.

Him! Just him. Not them!

He poured another generous slug into his champagne flute and sloppily waved the dark green bottle at the other man, silently asking if he wanted more.

The man ignored the gesture. "You knew I was investing the money that we had set aside for our daughter Marnie to attend medical school at McMaster's. You knew!" he shouted, spittle escaping his lips.

"Investments are never guaranteed," Quartermain said, then he tipped the glass up and greedily sucked in a mouthful. "Damn, that's good," he smacked his lips. "Too bad the fricking Frenchies have copyrighted the word *champagne*. This's," he remarked, waving his flute in front of the visitor, "an outstandin' champagne."

"You callous bastard! Talking about your damn wine when you've ruined my daughter's future. Our Marnie is gifted. She would have been a brilliant oncology surgeon." Holding his head in his hands the man sobbed, "It's gone. It's all gone. We can't afford to send her to any medical school at even the cheapest university."

"Oh, for god's sake stop your whining. I never guaranteed the 200% return on your investment. I said it was a poshibility," Quartermain slurred as his fingers made sarcastic air quotes. "If you had half a brain, you would have known that if it seems too good to be true, it really *is* too good to be true."

In a blur of motion, the older man reached for the heavy champagne-style bottle. Fueled by rage he slammed his makeshift weapon into Quartermain's head. Quartermain staggered, lifting his arms in an uncoordinated attempt to protect himself. The man struck again.

Quartermain moaned and fumbled to touch the fierce pain in his head but his knees folded and he sank to the floor. His eyes rolled back and he toppled over as he lost consciousness. He was dimly aware of a wet and hollow sound as his head struck the concrete.

The bottle held high over his head the assailant hesitated. *Oh god, oh god!* What have I done? He had only meant to reason with Quartermain, to see if he could somehow recoup his two hundred-and fifty-thousand-dollar investment. He sunk to his knees weeping.

Then, Quartermain groaned; he appeared to be coming around. The attacker knew he had no choice — he had to finish the job and make it look like an accident. He gripped Quartermain's shirt and jerked the unconscious but still breathing man toward the warehouse. A trail of blood smears followed the macabre procession.

Panting with exertion and fear, the man scanned the area. Vats, perhaps he could drown Quartermain in one. No, too difficult to drag the heavier man up the ladder and stuff him into a vat. A fall from the ladder? Or, a suicide? Quartermain was obliviously drunk. There were three empty bottles on the desk. Yes, that was it. In a drunken haze he'd had an attack of remorse and killed himself. The man rapidly searched the work area looking for anything that might be of use. He found a length of nylon rope hung on a peg.

Corked

He frantically scanned the area looking for something to hang Quartermain from and noticed the forklift. He ran toward it and jumped into the driver's seat. No keys. He hopped out and ran to the workbench, scrabbling at the mess of small tools and paperwork scattered on the worktop, then he spotted the keys hanging from a pegboard. He snatched them up and ran back to the machine and shoved them in the ignition. He jumped out and tightly tied a loop around Quartermain's neck, started the forklift, looped the rope around one of the forks and securely tied it. Leaping back into the driver's seat he lifted Quartermain until his toes were well clear of the floor, then watched in horror as he partially regained consciousness and clawed at the rope around his neck, his feet scrabbling uselessly in the air. Sobbing, the man snatched the keys from the ignition. As he stumbled past the workbench, he unconsciously replaced the keys on the pegboard.

"Marnie, sweetie, I am so sorry," he mumbled. *Her dream was in ashes. How was he going to explain to his wife that there would never be a Doctor Marnie in their family?*

The attacker searched the work area then grabbed a cloth and a bottle of muriatic acid. He scrubbed furiously at the trail of smears. Intuitively he knew that the crime scene technicians could find the blood with their high-tech tools and chemicals, but he fervently hoped that they wouldn't think to look in the wine shop. If he could establish an alibi perhaps the cops would look at someone else. His wife was his only hope. If he came clean with her and promised to work doubly hard to recoup the money, then maybe, just maybe, he would get away with this.

But that sound would stay in his brain forever. The thud of the bottle smashing into Quartermain's head, like his baseball bat mashing into a hollowed-out Halloween pumpkin when he was ten. Dashing for the staff washroom the man noisily puked into the toilet.

"What!" Her fists cocked on her skinny hips; his wife scowled at him. "What did you do?" It wasn't that she hadn't heard, she simply couldn't believe what she was hearing.

"I invested Marnie's tuition fees."

"All of it?"

"Yes, all of it."

"You fool! *Invested* it in the winery," she shouted. "More like flushed our money down the toilet."

"Shh, darling, please, we don't want the other hotel guests to hear us." He held his index finger to his lips, the other hand motioned for her to tone down the volume of her voice.

"I don't give a good god damn who hears us," she shrieked. "We agreed! No more than twenty-five thousand."

"I know, I know. But he promised a fantastic return on our money," the man whined.

"And you fell for it," she glared at him and shook her head. "Well, you will get our money back."

"I can't," he said. "the board of directors found out today that Quartermain has oversold the shares."

"By how much?"

"Two hundred percent."

"So, the shares are worthless," she stated. "You and the entire board of directors are the stupidest men on earth, believing that con man."

He bowed his head, and whispered, "There's more."

"Tell me."

Tears ran down his face. "I think I killed him." He swiped a hand under his nose, smearing tears and snot.

She put her hand over her mouth, and mutely stared at him.

Corked

"It was an accident, I swear," he sobbed as he sank to his knees. "You have to believe me."

Shaking her head as if to dislodge his confession from her memory, she asked, "What do you mean you *think* you killed him? How could you not know? What did the ambulance attendants say?" Her face was a mix of bewilderment and fury.

Terrified, he pinned his eyes on the floor, "I … I didn't call them."

She sank onto a chair. "What have you done?"

Chapter 14

Kelowna airport Okanagan

"Snow!" Jessica protested. "It doesn't usually snow here in March."

They were standing outside at the Kelowna airport, keys in hand and searching for the rental car they had reserved. She crossed her arms and hugged them close to her ribs, her sweater and light jacket weren't up to the job of keeping her warm. She was freezing. Fortunately, it wasn't the skin-burning cold that was common in January, but still there was a huge difference in temperatures between the tropical warmth of Isla Mujeres and the Canadian storm.

"It's a freak storm that arrived today," Mike said, checking his phone for details. "It's dumped a meter already, with more to come." He suppressed a shiver, "I don't have a winter coat, only my hoodie."

"And I have nothing to keep Sparky warm. The poor guy is vibrating he's so cold."

Mike pointed at a sign halfway through the parking lot. "Over there, that's where we pick up our car." He plunked the laptop on top of a suitcase and grabbed the handle of the two biggest cases, leaving Jessica to wrestle a smaller one and Sparky.

Keeping in the tire tracks, they slogged through the ankle-deep snow to the rental car parking area. Unrecognizable white mounds filled the parking lot. Mike hit the unlock on the remote control and was rewarded with a flash of lights from one of the lumps. "I guess that's our vehicle; does it look like a Hyundai Sonata to you?" he asked trudging toward the vehicle.

"Who can tell? It's just a pile of snow," Jessica answered.

When they reached the white mound that had responded to the bleep of the remote, Mike opened the trunk, shoved everything including the laptop inside, then knocked a pile of snow away from a back door and opened it. "In you go, Sparks," he said, hoisting him into the seat.

With a credit card in hand, Jessica was busy swooshing the fluffy snow off the windshield, then she scraped the underlying ice away.

"Catch," he said, tossing her the key fob. "Start it up and get the heat on." He located a long-handled brush under the seat, and went to work removing snow and ice from the other windows. He tossed the brush in the trunk, and slid into the passenger side of the sedan. "Do you know how to find our hotel?" he asked.

"Sure, that's easy," she said. She adjusted her seat position and checked the side mirrors. "I know Penticton is only an hour away, but I'm glad we are staying overnight here in Kelowna."

"Yep, me too. I'm tired, cold, and cranky," Mike agreed as he fastened his seatbelt. "This feels odd. I haven't worn a seatbelt since moving to Mexico last spring."

"I haven't used a seatbelt in years," Jessica said. "When we get to the hotel, I need to walk Sparky a bit before we go to bed."

"Too bad the little guy can't use our toilet."

"His legs are too short," Jessica said.

Mike laughed at her remark, then rubbed his hands together in an attempt to create a bit of warmth, "Let's get moving — I'm freezing," he said. "My blood has thinned out from living in Mexico."

"Me too." Jessica put the transmission in reverse and gently pushed on the gas pedal. The Sonata responded, sluggishly. As she accelerated up the ramp leading from the airport level to Highway 97, the vehicle fishtailed on the incline. "What the hell? We're sliding all over the place," she muttered at the unexpected movement.

"Doesn't it have winter tires?"

Corked

"You would think so, but it sure doesn't feel like it does." Clawing their way forward, they reached the highway and she turned south toward Kelowna. "At least this bit is plowed and sanded." She unclenched her fingers and relaxed slightly, "Tomorrow I'll call the rental company to exchange this one for another one with better tires. This is ridiculous."

The next morning as they packed up to leave the hotel Mike asked Jessica, "Did the rental company agree that we could exchange the Sonata for one with winter tires?"

"Not a chance. The customer service rep told me that only ten percent of their vehicles have snow tires, and they're all rented. We're out of luck."

"That's terrible service," he said.

"I know, but it is what it is," she agreed. "We'll just have to be careful, especially on the hills. The temperature is supposed go up in few days, and that'll melt the snow."

"Good, since we were originally headed to California, I'm not prepared for full-on winter," Mike said.

"Me either. Let's get checked out, grab some coffees, and head south to our hotel in Penticton."

"Sounds good. Am I driving or you?"

"I'll drive." She picked up the keys, wrapped Sparky's lead around her fist, and opened the room door. "Could you grab my bag, please? I've got Sparky's bag and him."

"Got it," Mike said pulling up the handles on the two bigger suitcases and squeezing past Jessica, who was holding the door open. "Remind me why Sparky needs his own bag."

"Doggie bed, food, water bowl, dishes, extra leash and harness."

"It's like traveling with a toddler," Mike groused good-naturedly.

"Exactly."

After checking out of the hotel, Jessica pointed the vehicle south on Highway 97. "Once we are over the bridge, we can grab coffees. I just want to get past the morning rush hour," she said.

Fifteen minutes later they crossed the famous William R. Bennett Bridge, with its sections of long, floating pontoons. In West Kelowna, they stopped for a supply of coffees and pastries, then continued south to the small, and charming lakeshore communities of Peachland, Summerland, and Penticton. The mostly four-lane highway followed the long shoreline of Okanagan Lake through hills covered in bunchgrass and sagebrush, and past slumbering orchards and dormant vineyards.

Mike turned his head from side to side, trying to take in the scenery. "What's with the miles of fencing?" He asked, pointing to first one side of the highway, and then the next.

"The tall fencing along the side of the highway is to keep the wildlife off the road, the fencing of individual properties is to protect the vineyards and fruit trees from hungry animals," Jessica said. "About twenty years ago, during a particularly bitter winter, there were thousands of mule deer killed and many people seriously injured in traffic accidents caused by the deer crossing the roadway looking for food and water."

"That's awful."

"It was horribly tragic for the humans and the animals," she agreed.

"Okay, this is our hotel." Jessica turned into the driveway, and parked under the covered entrance of the Ramada Hotel and Suites. She turned to Mike. "Your turn. I drove, you can sign us in."

"Yep," he agreed and hopped out. "I have us booked into a pet-friendly apartment for a month, then we can decide if we want to extend our stay here, or find something else."

She pulled Sparky inside the elevator. "Don't worry, little man. This is going to be a fun experience for you."

"Is this his first elevator ride?"

"Yep, and yesterday was his first plane ride."

"He's doing good so far," Mike said. "Monday is my first work day and once I am settled in, I'll see if we can find you a casual position helping out in the vineyards or perhaps the production area."

Jessica tipped her head to look at Mike. "All of your carefully thought-out plans went up in smoke."

"Yeah, a job for me, a job for you, and permission for Sparky to live with us in the complimentary guest cottage in lovely, warm California. Poof." He laid his hand on her smooth cheek. "Thank you for being so flexible."

"It'll cost you." Her eyes invited him closer.

"Anything," he murmured, lowering his head.

"A kiss," she whispered.

"Deal," he said kissing her thoroughly as the elevator doors opened.

"Nice," said a woman.

"Sorry about that," Jessica said with a cheeky grin, and stepped out with Sparky in tow.

"No need to apologise; I'm jealous," the woman answered with a smile as she entered the elevator.

"This is us," Mike said. He stopped in front of their room, and ran the key card through the slot and pushed open the door.

"Not bad," Jessica said, taking a quick tour of the one-bedroom apartment in the tower complex at the hotel. "Kitchen, sitting area, fireplace and a view of the golf course. It'll do nicely."

"After we unpack, I'd like to drive out to the winery just to have a look. It's about thirty minutes south of here, is that okay with you?" Mike asked.

"Sure, but what about the pooch?"

"Bring him along; he'll enjoy the ride," Mike said.

"Okay, but first we need to do a quick shop for winter jackets for all three of us," she said. "I did a quick search on the internet. There is an inexpensive clothing store and a good pet supply place in the same shopping mall at the south end of town. We should be able to get everything we need in the one spot."

"Sounds good; just tell me how to get there."

Chapter 15

Southern Okanagan Valley

"Stop. Quick, pull over," Jessica shouted to Mike.

"What's wrong?" He asked as he quickly scanned the road ahead, looking for a place to safely pull off the icy pavement.

"Sparky is sick," she said.

He steered the Sonata into a wide spot, away from the dirty white drifts piled by the grader along the side of the road. "Not having winter tires makes driving interesting," he said as the back end of the car lurched a foot to the right.

As soon as Mike stopped the vehicle and put the gearshift in park, she opened her door and got out. "He's puked all over the back seat."

"Nice," Mike said. "Did he get it on his new jacket?"

She opened the back passenger-side door and examined Sparky. "No, he missed that," Jessica said as she scanned his warm red coat. "I need something to clean up this mess."

"What about that thing he's sitting on?"

Jessica considered the new blanket that she had just bought to keep Sparky comfortable on the chilly upholstery. "It'll have to do. Move pooch, so that I can get the blanket," she said, tugging on one end.

"Why'd he get sick?"

"He's too short. He can't see out the windows and he's not used to a curvy road."

"But he enjoyed riding in your golf cart on Isla. Those roads are curvy," Mike said.

"Wind in his face. Ears flapping. And he could see where he was going." She mopped up the smelly goo, and rolled the blanket into a sausage shape. "Pop the trunk, and I'll stash this."

Jessica slid back into the passenger seat and patted her thigh. "Come on, little man, stand on my lap and look out." Sparky walked between the seats, and stood on Jessica's thighs. "He's a heavy little bugger," she said, shifting his weight so that it was more evenly distributed on her legs.

"All set then?" Mike asked.

"Yep, let's carry on."

Mike checked his mirrors, looked over his left shoulder and swung the sedan back onto the road.

A few minutes later Jessica spotted a herd of twenty or more bighorn sheep pawing the snow-covered grass by the side of the road, "Go slow, Mike; these guys are nervous. We don't want them scrambling over the hood of the car."

"Really? They can do that?" He said lifting his foot from the gas pedal and lightly tapped the brake.

"Yep, they can bounce a long way but sometimes they scrape the paint with their hooves."

Jessica fumbled in her pocket, extracting her tiny Nikon Coolpix and powered down her window. "Whoa, buddy," she grabbed at Sparky's collar with her left hand as he pushed his head and upper body out of the window to investigate the strange smelling animals.

"I'm surprised you use a camera. I thought everyone used their phones for photos," Mike said.

"It's small, fits in my pocket, and has a better lens than my phone," she said, pointing the camera at the closest ram.

Ellen Taylor pulled her keys out of her pocket to unlock the winery for the start of her work day. The door swung open. Puzzled, she walked inside and reached for the light switch, but the lights were already on.

"Hello? Anyone here?" She shouted into the echoey space.

Silence.

"Ben? Are you here?" She shouted for the cellar master. Trudging up the stairs to the second-floor office area, she dumped her purse in a drawer and switched on her computer. Leaving her coat on until her office was warmer, she tapped the thermostat a few degrees higher, picked up her coffee cup, and headed back downstairs to the ground level wine cellar. They had the best coffee, and maybe someone had arrived early and made a pot.

"Phew, what's that smell?" She said as she entered the tank room. She glanced toward the rows of stainless-steel tanks, towering over her in the gloomy interior. She reached out and flicked on more lights, and screamed. The large forklift sat in the middle of the warehouse, and the body of Kingsley Quartermain slowly twirled at the end of a rope that was looped over one of the metal forks. Ellen dashed toward the man and grasped his thigh. "Kingsley! Kingsley, can you hear me?" He was stiff and cool to the touch. Ellen fumbled with her phone, punching in 911.

Her voice shaking, she blurted into the phone, "We need an ambulance. *No Regrets Winery*. I think my boss is dead."

The soothing voice on the other end confirmed the address and assured her that emergency services were on the way.

Disconnecting the call, Ellen noticed that she was standing in a pool of dark, foul liquid that smelled like an overused outdoor toilet. She turned her head and upchucked her meager breakfast onto the concrete floor.

Jessica pointed at a sign, *No Regrets Winery and Vineyards*. "That looks like it."

"Yep, my new bosses. They hired me to bring the wines up to medal-winning status. Hopefully."

"Is that hopefully they've hired you or hopefully you can create medal-winning wines?"

"Careful, don't jinx this contract!" He stopped the vehicle, and they got out. "Should we put Sparky on his leash?"

"I don't imagine he's allowed inside. I'll give him a couple of minutes for a pee, then put him back in the car," Jessica said, at the same time a loud, frightened wail came from direction of the building.

"Something's happened," Mike ran toward the sound, with Jessica and Sparky hot on his heels. They barged through the open doors running past an assortment of equipment and boxes of bottles, toward the sobbing woman bowed over beside a forklift. The thin brunette wiped her mouth as she straightened up.

"Ma'am, can we help you?" Mike asked.

"Who are you?" she shrieked and backed away.

Mike held his hands palms out, showing her that he wasn't a threat, "I'm Mike Lyons, the consultant who starts work tomorrow. What's happening?"

The woman moved aside and pointed, "My boss," she said, and started to tremble. "Can we get him down? He might be alive."

Mike hopped into the driver's seat of the forklift. "No keys. Do you know where they are?"

The woman dashed to the corkboard beside the workbench, and picked up a keyring. "Here, these are the keys."

Mike started the forklift and lowered Quartermain to the floor. Jessica leaned over and felt his throat for a pulse, then shook her head. "I don't feel a pulse," she said, knowing that the hard flesh under her fingertips meant he was dead, and had been for several hours.

"I'm Jessica," Jessica said, as she straightened up and focused on the traumatized woman. "What's your name?"

"Ellen," the woman whispered, "Ellen Taylor, I'm the office manager." Her eyes were red-rimmed from crying, her face pinched and white with signs of shock.

"You need to sit down," Jessica said guiding her in the direction of a stool that was tucked under a wooden worktop. Ellen slumped onto the seat with her back turned toward the unmoving figure.

"Have you called 911, Ellen?" Mike asked.

"Yes, about five minutes ago," she said. "They should be here soon." With shaking hands Ellen punched the numbers for Matthew Douglas. Holding the phone against her ear her eyes nervously searched the cavernous space, unsure if Kingsley had committed suicide or if his killer was still in the wine cellar. Normally a noisy, busy work area, the space reverberated with an eerie silence.

"Douglas," he answered abruptly.

"This is Ellen. There's been a terrible tragedy here at the winery."

"What happened?"

"I'm not exactly sure, but I think Kingsley is dead."

"Dead?" Douglas gasped. "Have you called the police?"

"I called the ambulance, and the dispatcher said the police would come as well."

"Ambulance? I thought you said he was dead," sputtered Douglas.

"I think he's dead," she emphasized, "but I've called the ambulance just in case."

"I'll be there in twenty minutes," Douglas said and disconnected the call.

"That was rude," Ellen muttered to the phone.

Jessica raised an eyebrow, wondering what had been said. Then she glanced down and realized that Sparky was AWOL.

"Sparky?"

Chapter 16

No Regrets Winery

The two ambulance attendants hopped out of the unit and with a practiced tap of their hands shut the vehicle doors as they strode toward the back of the van. Flipping the release lever, they removed the stretcher, dropped and locked the wheels, then walked rapidly toward the imposing structure.

"What've we got?" asked the RCMP officer who arrived just seconds after them. The Royal Canadian Mounted Police were the federal force that provided policing across most of Canada.

"Possible death. Not certain."

"Has anyone called the coroner?"

"Not until we've assessed the situation."

The taller ambulance attendant pushed open the heavy wooden door. "Hello? Anyone here?"

"Over here," a shaky female voice replied.

The wheels of the metal stretcher clattered over the concrete floor, as the first responders headed in the direction of the woman's voice.

Corked

"He's there," she said, pointing.

The taller ambulance attendant lightly gripped her forearm as she attempted to stand. "Stay seated, please," he said.

Avoiding the puddle of fluids on the floor the police officer squatted and checked for a pulse then placed his hand on the man's thigh. "*Rigor mortis*," he said referring to the stiffening of a corpse after death.

"*Rigor* starts in the jaw and neck and moves downwards," the shorter ambulance attendant remarked, "If his lower extremities are in *rigor*, then best guess is he died anywhere from six to twelve hours ago."

"I'll call the coroner," the RCMP officer said to the attendant, then turned his attention to the woman. "My name is Constable Swan." He stepped away from the body and walked toward Ellen. "I'm very sorry ma'am, I have to ask you a few questions."

She glanced away and nodded glumly.

"Do you know the victim?"

"Yes, he is … was … my boss, Kingsley Quartermain. He's the president of our company."

"And your name is?"

"Ellen Taylor. I'm the office manager."

"Thank you." His hand reached for the talk switch on his mobile, "Constable Swan here," he said to the dispatcher. "We need the coroner to respond to *No Regrets Winery*," he said, nodding as he listened to the questions. "Yes, full *rigor*," he replied. "The name is Kingsley Quartermain, the president of the winery." Ending the conversation, Swan turned back to Ellen. "When was the last time you saw Mr. Quartermain?"

"Last night around seven thirty."

"Here, at the winery?"

"Yes, I left him to lock up and I went home," she replied. Her eyes were pointed at the floor, avoiding the constable's questioning gaze.

"How did he seem? What was his mood?"

"What do you mean?" Recalling her acrimonious conversation with Kingsley, Ellen felt a wave of heat sweep from her chest to her face.

"Did he seem despondent?"

"Kingsley? No, never," she asserted. She lifted her tear-filled eyes and met Swan's, then swiped a hand over her wet cheeks. "Are you absolutely sure he's dead?"

The dark brown eyes of the thirty-something cop softened, "Yes, ma'am, I'm sure." He turned to eyeball Jessica and Mike.

"And who are you?" he asked.

Striving for a neutral expression, Mike reached out his hand to the RCMP officer, "I'm Mike Lyons, I'm the new consultant. This is my friend Jessica Sanderson," he said.

"Constable Swan," The RCMP officer said, ignoring Mike's outstretched hand as he wrote this new information in his notebook. "Are you working today, Mr. Lyons?"

"No, actually we just arrived. I don't officially start until tomorrow," Unsure if he was being snubbed, or the man was being cautious because of the new virus, Mike lowered his hand and tucked his finger tips into the front pocket of his jeans.

Swan raised his eyes to Mike's. "Then why are you here?"

"Jessica and I wanted to have a quick look, to familiarize ourselves with the location."

"Did you touch anything?"

Mike exhaled, "Yes, actually we did," he admitted.

"You disturbed the evidence?"

Mike pointed at the forklift. "He was hanging from the forks when we got here. I lowered the mast so that we could check for signs of life."

"And what did you find?"

Jessica interjected, "I checked his carotid artery. There was no pulse and he appeared to be in full *rigor*."

Swan's eyes flicked to Jessica. "How would you know about *rigor*, Ms. ..." he glanced at his notes, "um... Sanderson?"

"My mother is an ER nurse, and my dad and two brothers are firefighters. Dinner discussions tend to be about their experiences," she said as she scanned the warehouse.

Swan grunted, then added, "Are you looking for something, Ms. Sanderson?"

"Yes, my dog, Sparky."

"A dog? Here? In the middle of my investigation?"

"He slipped away when I was helping Ellen," she said, pointing to the other woman. "I didn't realize he had disappeared until now. May I look for him?"

"No! Stay where you are. Call him."

"If he has found something that appeals to his sense of smell, he might not listen to me."

"Call him."

"Sparky, Sparky baby!" she yelled, and clapped her hands, then she shouted the Spanish phrase for come here, "Sparky, *iven aca!*" That command usually brought him running with a worried expression in his eyes and his tail tucked under his rump.

He peeked out from behind a tank, then deliberately moved back.

"Sparky, *iven aca!*" She repeated with more force. Once more he looked at her, then moved behind the tank.

"That's weird. Maybe we should see what he is interested in," she said to Swan. "He has a really good nose." She didn't elaborate on the number of crimes that Sparky had helped solve. She knew that most police officers were skeptical of the value of his assistance until they saw him in action and even then, sometimes their pride wouldn't allow them to admit that a mutt could be a good detective.

With a deep intake of air, Swan straightened his spine. "Only you," he said pointing a finger at Jessica. "You," he turned the same finger toward Mike, "stay here with Ms. Taylor. Don't move. Don't touch anything. Got it?"

"Yes," Mike resisted the urge to snap a salute and bellow *Yes Sir!*

"Come with me," Swan gestured at Jessica leading her around a row of tanks to where Sparky seemed to be hiding and away from the death scene. "Don't touch anything!"

"Got it," Jessica said, "Sparky? Where are you baby?"

"Why doesn't he bark to let you know where he is?"

"He just doesn't. He's very quiet unless someone is threatening me, or trying to break into our house."

Swan stopped suddenly and turned to look at her, "Does that happen often to you?"

Jessica jerked to a stop to avoid running into the man, "Ah, well, we lived in Mexico for several years."

"Where?"

"Isla Mujeres, the Island of Women."

"Es what?"

"EES-lah moo-HAI-r-r-r-ayce," she said rolling the r-sound with her tongue. "It's an island near Cancun."

"Cancun, I know where that is. There are a lot of cartel problems in and around that area," he said, his dark brown eyes scrutinizing her blue ones.

And now he's suspicious. Jessica could almost read the mental note he made, linking her name to the Cancun drug scene. "As long as you don't hang around with drug dealers or frequent the nightclubs that are the favorites of the cartel, it's quite safe. Especially in a small community like Isla Mujeres."

Swan huffed and then turned to walk to where the dog was last seen. "Hey, get away from that," he shouted at Sparky.

"What's wrong?"

"He's contaminating something that might be evidence."

Jessica moved her head get a better view, but she couldn't see what Sparky was so absorbed with, "Sparky, come here, baby." She stooped and patted her knees. This time he decided it was in his best interests to obey her. He scampered to her side and leaned in for a pat.

"I'll handle it from here," Swan said. "Take your dog outside and put him in your vehicle. And don't touch anything."

"Come on pooch," she slapped her thigh and whispered to Sparky, "and don't touch anything or you'll upset the nice policeman." Pretending she hadn't noticed Swan's glare, she retraced her path to where Mike was waiting. "The Sparkinator has been banished to the car. May I have the keys?"

Chapter 17

No Regrets Winery

Jessica partially lowered the two back windows to allow airflow. The temperature was right around freezing, but the sun had broken through the thick layer of lake cloud, and she didn't want to take any chances that Sparky might overheat. She bleeped the locks and reluctantly returned to where the others were. She knew at some point the investigators, more commonly known as detectives, would arrive. She didn't want to be caught up in yet another murder investigation, but since the keys weren't in the forklift ignition, this was probably a homicide rather than a suicide.

A dead person would have a difficult time climbing down from the raised forklift mast to return the keys to their spot on the pegboard.

As she pulled open the heavy wooden door, a plain white four-door sedan arrived. Pointedly disregarding the newcomers, she walked inside and joined Mike and Ellen at the workbench. "I think the detectives have arrived," she murmured. "Get set for more questions."

"But I've told them everything I know," Ellen protested. She nervously ran a hand through her thin hair, adding to her distressed appearance.

"I know, but they always want to hear the story firsthand from the witnesses."

"How do you know? Have you experienced something like this?" asked Ellen.

"Um, sort of," Jessica temporized, her eyes met Mike's. Just last month they had been enjoying a music event at an island fundraiser when the musician collapsed on the stage. Jessica and Mike had rushed to help, performing CPR until the ambulance attendants arrived and took over the resuscitation efforts. The man was pronounced dead at the scene by the local doctor. A few minutes later, as Sergeant Ramirez listened to their account of the incident, he had warned Mike about associating with Jessica. Ramirez contended that Jessica had been involved, in one way or another, with a number of suspicious deaths on the island. When she objected to his factitious remark, he had flashed a mocking smile at her and continued his investigation. Irritated, she knew better than to get into an argument with Ramirez. The Mexican policía were underpaid, undertrained, and for the most part *mucho-macho* males. And later, there had been the added complication of Ramirez repeatedly hitting on her, telling her he would be happy to show her a really good time. It was complicated, but yes, she did know something about suspicious deaths.

"Ms. Sanderson," Swan said, breaking into Jessica's thoughts. He was walking toward her, followed by a man and a woman dressed in casual clothing.

"Yes?" She noticed that since she had inadvertently mentioned that she lived in Mexico, Swan had been keenly scrutinizing her.

"This is Corporal Smith, General Investigative Section, GIS, of the Penticton RCMP," he said pointing at the tall woman dressed in black skinny jeans, mustard-yellow shirt, and a black winter jacket, "and this is Constable Jones," he said, indicating the younger man.

"Smith and Jones," Jessica said, unable to control the twitch of her lips as she swallowed a laugh. Smith had shoulder-length red hair, pale skin and a generous, but at the moment, unsmiling mouth. Jones with his short dark hair, deep dimples, and blue eyes was boy-band cute. She was surprised that he had a straight well-proportioned nose, one that hadn't been rearranged early on in his career by an unruly drunk.

"And this," Swan added, with a chill in his voice, "is Jessica Sanderson and Mike Lyons. Until recently they were residents of Mexico."

Corked

Smith's eyebrows popped up at the mention of Mexico, but her first question was of a personal nature: "Do our names amuse you, Ms. Sanderson?"

"*Alias Smith and Jones* was a television western that my parents enjoyed watching in the 1970s," Jessica answered.

Mike sighed, and dropped his chin.

"And you Mr. Lyons, what's your opinion of our names?" Smith asked.

"I have no opinion," he said with a slight shake of his head.

Smith studied Mike for a moment, glanced back at Jessica, then turned her attention to Ellen Taylor. "Constable Swan tells me that you found Mr. Quartermain this morning. Please tell me exactly what you saw and did."

"I've already told the other officer everything I know," Ellen demurred.

"Yes, I understand, but frequently we discover more details when the witnesses repeat their stories," Smith responded. "Now, please, from the beginning." She concentrated on listening to Ellen, while Jones recorded the conversation on his phone.

Reluctantly Ellen recounted the story of how she came to work, found the door unlocked and some of the lights on and when she switched on more lights, she saw Kingsley Quartermain and screamed. She pointed at Jessica and Mike. "Then they arrived and helped me."

"What did you do?" Smith asked Mike.

Mike said, "We were in the parking lot when we heard the scream. We ran inside, saw Ellen was distressed, and asked what was wrong. She pointed at the body. Jessica checked for a pulse. We asked Ellen if she had called 911, and she said she had." He glanced at Jessica. "Did I forget anything?"

"Yes, the part about lowering the forklift mast."

"Right. I hopped in the driver's seat and tried to lower the forks, but there weren't any keys in the ignition. Ellen found them on a pegboard and then I lowered the mast so that we could see if Mr. Quartermain was still alive."

"No keys in the ignition?"

"Correct."

Smith cut a look at her partner, indicating that bit of information was significant. He tipped his chin in acknowledgment, then scribbled a note.

"You handled the keys," Smith said, "and in the process smudged any previous fingerprints."

"We were trying to help Mr. Quartermain," Mike replied.

"Yes, of course." Smith turned to Jessica. "Anything else?"

Jessica briefly argued with herself, but her curiosity triumphed over caution, "My dog was very interested in something behind that tank," she said. "What did he find?"

"Dog?" Smith asked.

"Sparky was with us when we ran inside. He wandered off to explore an exciting smell. It's what he does best. He finds things." Jessica clamped her lips closed. *Shut up! You're babbling.*

"Did the dog find something, Constable Swan?"

"An old ballcap. I left it for the Forensic Identification Services to process, he said, referring to the RCMP equivalent of Crime Scene Investigators."

"Satisfied?" She arched a look at Jessica, then turned toward Swan. "Constable, do you have the contact information and cell phone numbers for the witnesses?" Smith asked.

"Yes, ma'am, I do."

"Ms. Sanderson and Mr. Lyons, you can go, for now," Smith said, "Ms. Taylor, we'll need to chat further with you. Perhaps in your office?"

Corked

Mike started the engine of the Sonata and put it in gear. The parking lot was a mix of snow-covered pavement and gravel, and he carefully eased away, taking care to not slide or spin the tires. He glanced at Jessica and shook his head; a little grin tweaked the corners of his mouth.

"What?" Jessica asked, then patted her thigh signaling Sparky to sit on her lap and look out the window.

"When it comes to cops, you just can't stop poking the bear."

"They're just people. Not gods."

"In your mind, not theirs."

"It's a coping mechanism. Everyone in my family, except me, works in emergency services. They use humor to deal with the death and devastation." She apprehensively turned her eyes to Mike. "Does that bother you?"

"I was a volunteer firefighter for a number of years so, I get it," Mike said, "but, maybe you could stop annoying every cop you meet." He squeezed her hand and winked at her.

Chapter 18

No Regrets Winery

Ellen perched nervously on the edge of her chair, waiting for Smith to continue with her questions.

"How are you doing, Ms. Taylor? Can we make you a cup of coffee or perhaps a cup of tea?" Smith asked.

"I'll be fine. Let's just get this over with please," Ellen's vibrating hands contradicted her statement that she was fine.

"All right, what can you tell me about your boss, Kingsley Quartermain?"

"What do you mean?" Ellen's stomach cramped at the thought of the financial mess Quartermain had created.

"Married? Children? Age?"

"Oh, well, he was married and they have two small daughters, but he and his wife recently split. I think he is … was forty-two years old."

"Where does Mrs. Quartermain live? We'll have to notify her as soon as possible," Smith said.

"She's taken the children and returned to her family in Alberta," Ellen replied.

"Was it a difficult separation?"

"I don't know. I didn't know Alison very well," That was the truth, while she didn't know Alison well, she knew the separation was loud and messy, having overheard several fights in Kingsley office. His marriage troubles weren't her concern.

"We'll need her contact information," Smith said.

"Yes, of course," Ellen said as she shook the computer mouse awake, and searched for the file containing staff and family information. She recited the information to Smith.

"How about Mr. Quartermain's relationship with employees and suppliers?"

"Everything was fine."

Smith folded her arms across her chest and quietly studied Ellen, as if she was trying to read more into her statement, "Ms. Taylor, I have the feeling that you aren't telling us everything. This is quite possibly a murder. You don't want to be charged with obstructing the investigation, do you?"

"Ellen," boomed a loud voice, "where are you?"

"Here, Mr. Douglas," she shouted down the stairway, relieved for once to hear his abrasive tone, "upstairs in the office." Turning to the police detective, she said, "Mr. Douglas is the chairman of the board of directors. You should ask him about Mr. Quartermain.

"Ellen, what's going on?" Douglas said, as he entered the administration office and noticed Ellen in a staring contest with two strangers. "Who are these people?" he demanded.

"Mr. Douglas, this is Corporal Smith and Constable Jones, of the General Investigative Section, GIS, of the Penticton RCMP," Ellen waved a hand toward the others.

Douglas slowed his step and considered the officers, "An investigator? Isn't that unusual for a suicide?" he asked.

Smith tilted her head in his direction. "Who told you it was a suicide, Mr. Douglas?"

"I, uh, well, Ellen must have told me that." He looked at her for confirmation.

Smith swivelled her head back to Ellen, "Did you?"

"I don't remember what I said," she lied. "I was upset and scared." She knew exactly what she had said: "There's been a terrible tragedy here at the winery. She never mentioned suicide or homicide but she wasn't going to contradict Douglas.

"Scared? Why?"

"I don't remember why. I just remember I was scared and feeling sick," she said. "I threw up my breakfast."

"I see," Smith said, then pinged her scrutiny back to Douglas. "What can you tell me about Mr. Quartermain?"

"He was our company president until yesterday," Douglas said.

"Was he moving to another position?"

"Not that I know of."

Smith remained silent; her eyes fastened on Douglas's.

"Well, not at this winery. The board of directors and I decided to let Mr. Quartermain go."

"What was the reason for his dismissal?"

Douglas glared back, a mulish expression on his face. "I don't see how that has anything to do with this tragedy."

"Mr. Douglas, there is evidence that this was not a suicide, but a homicide. Now, please, why was Mr. Quartermain fired as president?"

"Financial misappropriation."

"Embezzlement. Stealing."

"There are a few discrepancies that we are sorting out," he retorted.

"We will need the names and contact information for everyone on the board of directors, including you."

"You can't possibly think that I, or anyone on the board, would be responsible for taking a life?" Douglas's voice rose to an indignant squeak. Ellen clamped her lips shut, and busied herself with printing the entire list of investors from her computer, then she took a pen and marked the names of the directors.

"This is the complete list. I have highlighted the directors including Mr. Douglas," she said, handing the paper to Smith. Her eyes skittered past Douglas's glare.

"And these other names?"

"Shareholders in the winery."

"So, everyone on this list was affected by the president's indiscretions?" Smith asked, tallying the number at around fifty names.

"I wouldn't know," Ellen replied.

"Mr. Douglas?"

"What?"

"Have all of these people been affected?"

"Well, yes, I suppose so," he said evasively.

"When did you find out there was a problem?"

Douglas stared at Smith. "Yesterday."

"Do all of the shareholders know?"

"Yes, we told everyone yesterday as soon as we found out."

Ellen remained silent. She was certain he and the other directors knew at least a day before the meeting, but the other investors had only been told yesterday. *Doesn't anyone tell the truth in this company?*

Smith said to Douglas, "This is a large pool of suspects. Do you know of any one person who appeared to be more upset than the others?"

"I can't think of anyone," Douglas temporized.

Smith glanced at the sheet, noting that each person's investment in the winery was listed next to their names. *Douglas, half a million dollars. That made him the largest shareholder, and now, her top pick as a person of interest.*

Smith examined Douglas more closely: late fifties or early sixties and carrying a bit more weight around his middle than he should but otherwise he looked reasonably fit and healthy. Still, overwhelming a younger, stronger man who appeared to be at least four inches taller than Douglas — that would be difficult. Unless Quartermain had been incapacitated somehow. The autopsy would give her more information, but a tox screen for drugs could take up to another two weeks, and in the meantime her boss would be riding her ass to solve the murder.

As soon as they finished their discussions with the staff, she was going to FaceTime a friend who had recently retired from the force. Calvin Adair, had done his twenty-five years of service with the RCMP and had retired to the same tiny island that Jessica Sanderson and Mike Lyons were from. It was a bit of information that Smith planned to keep to herself until she had a chance to speak with Calvin. *What a funny and very small world.*

Chapter 19

FaceTime call

"Hey Red, how's it goin'?" Smith said, calling her friend by his nickname. He was the classic Celtic ginger with pale skin, reddish hair that with age had faded to an off-white, and he had light-colored eyes.

Once handsome and smooth skinned, time had weathered Calvin's face to a collection of lumps, wrinkles, and a spade shaped nose that had been flattened several times. Wide-shouldered and stocky, the younger Calvin had been quick with his fists; now he was mellow and laughed a lot.

"I'm good Caitlin, how about you?"

"Everything's good here. Your beard is new," Caitlin gestured as if she was stroking facial hair, "with the shorts and colorful shirt, you could be a Caribbean Santa Claus." She placed one boot heel on her desk, then the other, crossing her ankles and leaning back in her office chair. Her tablet rested against her raised thighs.

"Yep, I do that at Christmas time. The local kids love it," he ran his hand over the curly white beard.

"I was under the impression that Santa wasn't a big deal in Mexico, that the Night of the Three Kings on January 6th was the gift night."

"That's true," Calvin agreed, "but with so many Canadians and Americans living on the island the kids have figured out they can get two sets of presents. Some on Christmas Day and more on the Night of the Kings."

"Kids are quick to pick up on stuff like that," she agreed. "Is Marie enjoying retirement?"

"She is. She's become involved with the scholarship program for island students, the diabetes clinics, and the two animal rescue groups. I hardly see her," Adair said.

"What're you doing to keep busy?"

"Deep sea fishing, a bit of puttering around the house, meeting with friends at our favorite bar in the evenings, and helping Marie with whatever she's got going."

"I'm jealous," Smith said, "Hey, do you know Jessica Sanderson and Mike Lyons? They lived on Isla Mujeres until very recently."

"I know Jessica better than her new boyfriend, Mike Lyons. She's been here longer. What's up?"

"I'm investigating a murder at a local winery and they just happened to be at the scene of the crime when I arrived."

Adair tipped his head back and his laughter boomed from her phone, "With a short, black and white mutt by the name of Sparky?"

"Yes. How did you know?"

"You'll have your hands full with Jessica. She is something of a legend around here. Sparky and Jessica have solved four or maybe five murders."

"Are you kidding?" Smith asked.

"No, I'm not."

"Does she have some type of police training or experience?"

"No, she's worked for a number of years as a waitress at *Loco Lobo*, and yet somehow she has become entangled in several murders in this area."

"Was she cleared in all of the cases?"

"Yes, including the kidnapping of her boss and the death of a Cancun cartel kingpin."

"Wait! She's involved with the cartels?" Smith said, as a shiver of excitement scurried up her spine. Maybe Constable Swan was onto something after all. Swan was a homebody, rarely traveling anywhere outside of Canada, so meeting a beautiful woman who had lived for several years in an area controlled by the cartel had titillated his imagination. Caitlin hadn't paid much attention to his theory, but maybe she was wrong, not Swan. "Tell me about that," she said to Adair.

"Not involved exactly, more like caught up in a mess. The kingpin was obsessed with her. He died, she survived."

"Red, details!"

"That would take an hour and Marie wants me to go to the grocery store," Adair replied. "You know, the honey-do list. Can I pop you an email when I get back with the links to several news articles? Would that work for you?"

"Okay. I would appreciate that."

"Oh, I almost forgot, Jessica and her best friend Yasmin Medina uncovered a pirate's treasure cache on the island."

"You're making this up. A pirate's treasure?" Smith said.

"Honest to god's truth," Adair held up one hand as if he was swearing an oath. "It was buried at the Hacienda Mundaca, in the middle of the island. A property owned by the famous pirate Fermin Mundaca."

"Then she's rich," Smith stated.

"Nope. The Mexican government took it all, without so much as a thank you for finding it."

"Huh. That would be really annoying."

135

Corked

"I'm sure it was, but the alternative was jail time."

"So, she did break the law?"

"No, not exactly, just bent it a bit," Adair said. "Jessica and Yasmin were following rumors and searching without the proper permits, but the permits are impossible to get so they just went ahead and did it anyway. Then when the officials found out that the two women had actually located the long-lost plunder, they gave them a choice: hand over the treasure or go to jail."

He turned his head, and reached out a hand, "I really have to wrap this up. Marie has just handed me the list of groceries she wants me to get," Adair said.

"Okay, thanks Red, please give Marie a hug for me."

"Hi, Caitlin," a female voice said as Marie leaned into view on the FaceTime call.

"Hi, Marie, so good to see you. Are you keeping this reprobate under control?"

"Sort of," Marie turned to wink at her husband. "He is taking this tropical island retirement to heart. Sun, sand, cervesa, and occasionally he does a few chores around the house."

"Any impact on you with this COVID-19 virus that has sprung up?" Smith asked.

136

"A little. The part-time residents are getting worried and are returning to their northern homes sooner than planned. So far, not too bad. How about you?" Marie asked.

"Everyone is worried, but not too much else has happened," Smith replied. "I'll let you go. Love to both. Bye for now." Smith leaned back in her office chair. She had a nosy amateur sleuth to deal with. *Wasn't that just special.*

Chapter 20

Penticton

Setting the grocery bags on the floor, Jessica bent and unclipped Sparky's leash and removed his new jacket, "All right, bud, give me a few minutes to put the groceries away and then I'll get you some food." She kicked off her wet boots, hung up her coat and then removed the dark blue pashmina from her neck, and draped it over the same hanger.

"Mike?"

"Yep?"

She could hear the toilet flush and then the tap running.

"What do you feel like doing for dinner?" She hollered as she padded across the galley kitchen to the refrigerator. "Do you want to go out, or order in?"

He sauntered out of the bedroom, "Sorry about leaving you with Sparky and the rest of the groceries. I was desperate to take a leak."

"You were running pretty fast for the elevator," she said smiling at him. "We managed." She propped the refrigerator door open with one knee and started to stack their purchases inside.

Mike eyed the food that she was unpacking. "Didn't we buy food for dinner?"

"This is the basics for breakfast," she said, "coffee, eggs, butter, milk, yogurt, bread. Nothing interesting."

"Do you want to go out then?"

"Sure, or we can order in."

"Nah, let's go out. I haven't seen much of the city yet."

"It's not that big, the population is around thirty-three thousand give or take a few hundred," Jessica said. "We drove through it this afternoon."

"True, but we didn't explore, we just drove through."

"Explore," she said with a little nod, "that won't take long."

Mike handed her the remaining items that needed to be refrigerated, "How do you know all this? Did you live here?"

"I lived and worked here the summer I graduated from high school. It was, and probably still is, the party city for the eighteen to twenty-five crowd. I'm friends on social media with some of the locals that I met that year," she said. She pulled two beers from the shelf, shut the refrigerator. "*¿Cerveza?*"

"*Si, gracias,*" he answered, then chuckled, "that's a reflexive response."

"What? That you wanted a beer, or you said yes in Spanish?"

"Both," he said. "Tell me more about Penticton."

"The downtown core isn't all that big, but with the influx of expansive wineries in the valley there is a higher level of disposable income. Many of the wine aficionados have the money to support an active arts community."

"What else brings people to the valley?" He rubbed Sparky's ears, then asked him, "You hungry little man?" The dog's tail swished on the floor.

Smiling at the affectionate interaction between Mike and Sparky, Jessica said, "mash this up with a handful of the kibble." She handed Mike a container of the lamb flavored high-end food the pet store manager had guaranteed would please her finicky pooch. Maybe she wouldn't have to worry about cooking Sparky the usual mix of chicken, rice, and supplements if his digestive system could tolerate this brand.

Jessica took another sip of the beer and thought about Mike's previous question. "Let's see, the orchards with their fresh peaches, cherries, apples, and plums are still a big draw. Festivals celebrating wine, micro-brewed beer, cider, jazz, collector cars, and dragon boats. Outdoor activities are huge too. Things like rock climbing, hiking, cycling tours, and endurance races." She moved to the table and pulled out a chair, "you've probably heard of the Ironman Triathlon, right?"

Mike placed the dish of food on the floor, "Sure have. The contestants swim, bike, and run all in the same day. I've heard it's a grueling race, and some of the contestants don't finish before the midnight deadline."

"It is a tough race, and this course is a favorite of the participants. In 1983, the city hosted the first Ironman North American and continued to do so until the race was moved in 2012 to Whistler BC," she explained. "And this year, it's scheduled to return to Penticton. Everyone is super excited about that, but because of COVID-19 it will probably be postponed."

Mike leaned against the kitchen counter, watching in amusement as Sparky thoroughly sniffed his food before sampling a small amount. "He acts like I'm trying to poison him."

"Pretty much," Jessica agreed. Sparky grudgingly removed another mouthful from the plate and ate it. "If the weather ever warms up to something that my tropical blood can endure, I'd like to try a new sport that I recently heard about."

141

"What's that?"

"Disc golf."

"Never heard of it. How do you play?"

"There are specific rules, but basically the players walk a challenging course and toss specially designed Frisbees into large baskets. Low score wins, like golf," Jessica said. "It's great exercise, there's no entrance fee, and Sparky is allowed to be with us."

"Sure, I'm game to try, if I don't die of hypothermia first," Mike reached down to retrieve Sparky's empty dish. He put it in the sink and ran hot water and a little dish soap over it. "I never thought I'd have such a hard time re-adjusting to frigid temperatures."

"Me too, although I lived in Mexico for five years, you were only there for nine months."

"Are you saying that I'm delicate, fragile?"

"Maybe, a little."

He bent and playfully kissed her. "What about the murder at the winery, how do you think that's going to play out with the locals?" he asked.

"It will be the hot topic for months. This isn't a violent city, homicides are still a rare occurrence," she said. "Last year a man killed four people in a dispute between neighbors and it still hits the news updates on a regular basis." She tipped back the bottle and emptied the last mouthful.

"I wonder if this murder is on the news yet?" Mike said. "Turn on the TV, and I'll grab us a couple more beers."

"I thought you wanted to go out and explore the city."

"*Mañana*," he said, using the well-known Spanish word with multiple meanings. It could mean the morning, or tomorrow, or the day after tomorrow, or if spoken as *mañana mañana* it could mean whenever or never. "Tonight, I just want to snuggle with my sweetie and the famous fuzz-butt. We can order in."

Chapter 21

Penticton

Caitlin Smith flipped on the hall light as she entered her townhouse, yelling, "Hi honey. I'm home."

A small black cat with a triangular patch of white on her chest blinked, stretched, and jumped off the sofa, then strolled toward the kitchen.

"Hungry?" Smith asked Tickle the Terrible.

Tickle was an ungrateful humane society rescue that slashed Smith's hands whenever they strayed too close to her soft and appealing tummy. The cat had once pooped smack dab in the middle of her windshield, after she had accidentally locked Tickle in the garage overnight. Why she loved this cat, she had no idea. Maybe it was Tickle's fiercely independent nature that appealed to her.

"What have you been up to today?" Smith wriggled out of her winter jacket, and tossed her purse on the kitchen counter. She reached inside a cupboard for a can of salmon flavored Fancy Feast, and scooped it out onto a small white plate then set it in front of Tickle. The cat sniffed the offering, turned disdainful yellow eyes on Smith, then flicked her tail and walked away.

"Not what you had in mind, Princess?" Smith asked. "You might want to reconsider your decision. I'm the only one in this house who has opposable thumbs, and therefore the only one with the ability to open a can of food for Your Highness," she said, then reached into the refrigerator and pulled out a can of locally brewed Naramata Nut Brown Ale.

Pouring the dark brown ale into a tall glass, Smith tapped the laptop mouse to wake up the computer. "All right, let's see what Calvin has to say about the infamous Jessica Sanderson," Smith said as she placed the laptop on her coffee table and settled onto her sofa. Tickle joined her, and allowed Smith to gently stroke her head and spine with her free hand.

Smith skimmed the email, then clicked on the various links to news articles involving Jessica Sanderson and her friend Yasmin Medina. The women had been busy: treasure hunting, avoiding kidnappings, finding bodies, and rescuing several young Cuban women who were headed for the North American sex trade. And it had been Jessica and Sparky who had recently solved the murder of a second-tier Nashville musician.

"God, this is worse than I thought," Smith groused, "a well-known amateur detective, and her

145

mutt, sticking her nose into my murder investigation."

She shifted the cat from her lap, and stood up. "If you aren't going to eat your dinner, Tickle, maybe I will," she said, walking toward her kitchen. The cat ignored her threat; she knew Smith would cave into her silent demands for a different flavor.

Opening the refrigerator door, Smith contemplated the meager offerings inside. She sniffed the various containers of takeout food, and decided the chicken vindaloo was the freshest choice. She poked at the contents, then dumped the food onto a plate and shoved it into the microwave for two minutes. While she waited for her food, she poured another can of the craft ale into her glass, set it on the table along with a placemat, utensils, and colorful paper napkin. Gourmet dining.

With her recent promotion, she had been transferred from the larger city of Winnipeg to the Penticton RCMP detachment. Geographically, Penticton was easy to navigate, but socially she was still finding her way around. The singles scene in the smaller city was practically non-existent, and everyone was naturally cautious around new police officers until they had time to get to know them. Being an unattached cop had it challenges, but being an unattached, female cop who had an imposing title was doubly intimidating for many men. And she was tall, taller than a lot of her male friends, which made dating even more of a challenge. She was lonely, damn lonely.

Until quite recently most members of the RCMP were expected to transfer to a different town or city every two years. It was the federal police force's policy designed to maintain a professional distance from the people that they were in charge of policing. That rule had been relaxed somewhat because of rising real estate prices. Most of the members who were transferred into the hot Vancouver real estate market couldn't afford to purchase a home and finding police officers who would accept the transfer, and not quit, had become problematic. With roots reaching back to 1873, the previously male-dominated organization had been forced to grudgingly adapt to changing times, allowing members to remain in their communities for longer rotations.

Fortunately, when she was advised of her promotion and transfer, she had lucked into this two-bedroom, two-bathroom townhouse in a quiet cul de sac in Penticton. It had been an estate sale; the elderly woman had passed away in her bed. Caitlin didn't have any qualms about living in a house where someone had died. It was life. People died and frequently they died in a messy manner. Her occupation as an investigator brought her up close and personal with death. In the quiet of the night ghosts of past victims visited, reminding her that she had a moral obligation to solve their murder. Sleep was elusive most nights unless she self-medicated with a sleeping pill, or a few shots of single-malt whiskey.

Tonight might be one of those nights.

Her cell phone vibrated and danced on the kitchen table, demanding her attention. Putting her fork down, she picked up the device and swept a finger across the screen, "Smith here."

"Good evening Caitlin. This is Liz," Doctor Elizabeth Kennedy, the morgue pathologist, greeted her friend. "I've finished the preliminary examination of Mr. Quartermain."

"Hi Liz, anything noteworthy?"

"Yes, I've discovered two head injuries."

"Seriously? I can't believe I didn't notice," Smith said.

"They were hidden by his thick hair. He's been forcefully struck at least twice with a heavy object," the pathologist said, "but the bleeding had stopped by the time he was hung from the forklift."

"There wasn't any blood where we found him so we didn't look at the entire facility," Smith said. "I'll go back and search again."

"You'll need the FIS techs too."

"Yep, and my partner. They'll all be thrilled," Smith said. "Any idea of what type of weapon we're looking for?"

"Not exactly, but the indents appear to be made by a rounded object," the pathologist said.

"Perhaps a bottle?" Smith asked.

"Normally a bottle will break when used as a weapon."

Smith picked up her plate, and set it on the counter. Dinner, such as it was, was now over. She eyed her cat, wondering if she should dump the remaining vindaloo in the garbage or hope that Tickle wouldn't eat it. The spices could make the Tickle sick and cleaning up cat puke was not her favorite housekeeping task. She put the phone on speaker so that she could continue to talk to Liz, then opened the under-sink cupboard and scraped the remains into the bin. She ran hot water over the plate, rinsing off the residue then left it in the sink. One plate, one knife, one fork, and one glass didn't justify her using the dishwasher.

"Okay, thanks for the information, Liz. I've gotta call my partner and ruin his plans for dinner with his wife."

"Caitlin, wait," Liz said, "I just remembered. *No Regrets* makes a popular champagne-style wine. Those bottles are thicker, and designed to withstand the pressure of fermentation as it creates the bubbles," the pathologist said. "That might be a possibility as a murder weapon."

"Okay, thanks. I'll let you know what I find," Smith said, as she ended the call.

Reaching for her keys she glanced longingly at a bottle of Laphroaig single-malt. Not right now, there was more work to be done.

She checked the time and opened her phone contacts, "Hey E-Man," she said using Ethan Jones' nickname. "We've got a situation. Meet me at *No Regrets*, ASAP." Ignoring his moan of protest that his wife had just put his dinner on the table, Smith added, "I'll call FIS from the scene."

Disconnecting, she next tried the main phone number for the winery. "Hopefully someone is still working," she mumbled to herself.

Chapter 22

No Regrets Winery

"Police, open up," Smith thumped her gloved fist against the locked door. Her phone calls to Ellen Taylor, Matthew Douglas, and the main office number had all gone to voicemail but the lights were on in the warehouse and there was a mud-splattered Chevy pickup in the parking lot. It was positioned at the far end of the lot, in an area designated for staff vehicles. Someone must be working late.

"Police!"

"Hold on, don't get your panties in a twist," a male voice countered. The lock clicked and the door opened. "What's up?" He asked. "I thought the cops were finished here."

Smith took in the well-built thirty-something man blocking the doorway. He was about her height, although her thick-soled boots added another inch to her actual size. "Corporal Smith," she said holding open a thin wallet at eye-level; one side contained her RCMP badge, the other side her photo identification. "I need to search the crime scene."

He smirked and placed one hand on the door frame. "Don't you need a warrant or something?"

Squaring her stance, Smith stared at him. The scruffy black beard touching his breast-bone detracted from his brilliant blue eyes, straight nose, and thick eyebrows. With a bit of grooming the guy could be downright handsome, but trimming his beard wouldn't fix his cocky attitude. "This is a crime scene that I haven't released. I do not need a warrant to search the original area," she emphasised. "Please, step back." Holding his gaze, she pushed the right side of her thick jacket open, revealing the revolver that rested on her hip. Her eyebrows lifted, asking if he was going to cooperate, or to obstruct her.

"Whoa, no need to get cranky," he said, stepping backwards and leaving the door wide open.

Moving inside, Smith asked, "What's your name? And what do you do at the winery?"

"Ben, I'm the cellar master."

"May I see some identification please?"

"Jesus, you're a cranky bitc … person," he hastily corrected when he clocked her expression. He meekly reached into his back pocket for his wallet, pulled out his driver's licence and handed it to Smith.

She looked at his birthday date, born in 1989, then compared the photo to the man. It was the same face, but without the scruffy beard and she had guessed correctly; he was very good-looking under that mess of facial hair. "So, Ben Whitaker, how long have you worked here?"

He looked away and appeared to be mentally counting the months on his fingers. "About a year," he finally answered.

Perhaps he had run out of fingers, Smith mused. "What does a cellar master do?" She asked as she handed back his identification.

He shoved his wallet into his back pocket. "I'm the grunt who does all the hard, messy work so the self-important winemaker can take the credit." His lips twisted in a resentful expression. "Pick grapes, crush 'em, filter the juice, tank it, clean equipment, bottle wine. Anything and everything."

Smith had a basic understanding of the industry but wasn't precisely certain on the details. She had moved from a city with zero vineyards to the Okanagan Valley that had at least three hundred in operation and more under construction. How they all made enough money to stay in business was beyond her comprehension.

"And where were you last night?" She scrutinized his face.

"Am I a suspect?"

"Everyone is a suspect until we find our killer," she said, "so, again, where were you?"

"It was my day off. I was with my girlfriend, Suzanne."

"Will she corroborate your alibi when I contact her?"

"Yes, of course she will."

"Full name, address and phone number for you, and the same for your girlfriend," Smith said, handing him her pen and notebook.

He huffed, then wrote the information, and handed the notebook back to her.

"All right let's have a look." She indicated with her right hand that Whitaker should walk into the warehouse. He slouched ahead of her.

"Who removed the tape?" she demanded, pointing at one side of the squared-off area that Jones had cordoned off earlier in the day. The tape had been detached and draped over a what looked like a portable pump.

"I've got work to do," Whitaker said. "It's in my way."

Smith fumed. "The big black letters — do not enter — printed repeatedly on bright yellow tape didn't tell you anything?"

"I thought you were finished and just forgot to remove the stupid tape," he whined.

"Right. What else have you disturbed?"

"Nothing."

"I need to search all of the garbage cans and trash barrels. Show me please."

He pointed at the plastic container under the worktop. "That's the only one we have in here."

"When was it emptied?" She asked peering at the lone paper coffee cup.

"I don't know," he said, slouching against a large wooden pillar, "it was empty when I tossed my cup."

Behaving like a spoiled teenager, the guy was shredding her patience. She sucked in a breath, envisioned giving him swift kick in the ass and instantly felt better. "All right, take me to the wine shop."

"That's not part of the crime scene," he objected. "I could get in trouble with the boss."

"Take me to the wine shop," she repeated testily, "then call your boss. I've tried, and can't reach anyone."

"Fine." He clumped through a doorway and stopped at a carved wooden door. Whitaker unlocked the door and stepped inside then flicked the light switch. "I don't see anything," he said.

Standing behind him, Smith rolled her eyes at his inane comment. "Please, step outside and call your boss. I'll deal with this." She waited until he moved aside, then she crouched and examined the floor: dark brown tiles, with dark brown or perhaps dirt-encrusted grout. *The perfect color match for dried blood.*

She swiped the screen of her phone, opening up the contacts and called dispatch. "Corporal Smith here. I'm at *No Regrets Winery* and need to recall FIS," she said, then listened responded to the questions. "Yes, I have new information from Doctor Kennedy. Yes. Okay, twenty minutes. Thank you."

"Smith," Jones shouted from the main entrance, "where are you?"

"In here," she shouted back, "the wine shop."

She heard his boots thumping on the floor as he walked toward the sound of her voice.

"You know I was just about to eat my dinner, right?"

"Yes, I know," she agreed. "What gourmet delight did Meaghan create for your dining pleasure this evening?"

"My favorite. *Fajitas*, made with strips of charcoal-grilled steak, fresh *pico de gallo*, sauteed peppers and onions, sliced limes, warm tortillas and her special baked beans." He rubbed a hand over his flat stomach.

Smith dropped her chin and shook her head. "Ethan, I didn't ask for an ingredient list. I was being polite."

"But I love Mexican food," he moaned.

"Fantastic. You can swap recipes with our witness Jessica Sanderson. She lived in Mexico for several years," she retorted. "Now, can we please get to work?"

"Sure. What are we looking for?"

"The murder weapon," Smith said. "Liz Kennedy thinks the weapon is something curved, possibly a bottle, or more specifically a champagne bottle. I've already called FIS. They should be here shortly." She pointed at the floor. "Those stains in the grout could be dirt, or they could be dried blood. I can't tell."

The FIS tech turned to Smith. "There," she said, pointing at the patch illuminated by the luminol.

"Blood, and quite a bit of it."

"It's soaked into the grout and even though someone has attempted to clean it with an acid, it's still visible."

"Smith, look what I've found," Jones said. He held up a heavy bottle champagne with his gloved fingers.

"Where did you find it?"

"In the garbage bin out back, on the crush pad," he motioned with his head to the rear of the building.

"Good job," Smith said, "and I assume the crush pad has something to do with crushing grapes and not a person's head."

"You assume correctly," Jones agreed.

"Any sign of blood on the bottle?" she asked.

"None that I can see, but I did find a garbage bag with handfuls of bloody paper towels and a blood-soaked rag," he said. "I've bagged and tagged it as evidence."

"It looks like you had to climb in and dig around." Smith nodded at his soiled footwear.

"Leftovers from their annual shareholders dinner." He held up one foot and inspected the gunk that was mashed between the treads.

"Mmmm, that looks tasty," the tech joked. She held out a large evidence bag. "Put the bottle in here. I doubt we'll find much on it. The assailant has probably wiped it down as well, but hopefully we can confirm this is the murder weapon."

"Did you find any fingerprints?" Jones asked the tech.

"If you mean in the wine shop, yes, hundreds or maybe thousands of prints. It's a popular location for wine purchases," the tech said. "Some of the prints could be our killer but until we find something to match them to, they're useless." She looked at Smith. "I'm finished in there. Anything else you need?"

"What about the baseball cap the dog found in the warehouse. Anything I should know about?"

"I don't know anything about that. Check with my boss."

Chapter 23

Penticton

"Your first official day at the winery," Jessica wrapped her arms around Mike and gave him a long, lingering kiss. "Mmmm, you are very sexy in those snug jeans and manly work boots," she said as her hands strayed lower.

Mike leaned back and locked eyes with her, then asked in a serious tone, "And what about my red and black lumberjack shirt," he asked. "Don't you think that's sexy too?"

She pretended she was giving his question serious consideration before answering, "Yes, you're definitely a hottie in that shirt." She nibbled his lips, then released her hold.

Mike plucked at his crotch. "You make it difficult for me to walk properly, you know," he said resettling his equipment in his jeans.

Watching Mike shrug into a down-filled vest, Jessica smiled. "A little bump in your heart rate is good for your health. I know, because you give me heart-bumps every time you look at me."

"Good, don't ever lose that feeling," he leaned in for a quick kiss, then jammed his knitted cap on his head. "Can you keep an eye out for a Fed-Ex package? Pop shipped the winter clothes that I had stored at their house. They should be here soon," he said.

"The package will probably be left at the reception desk, but I'll keep an eye out for it."

"Okay, great. What're you and The Sparkinator going to do today?"

"Go for a walk. Catch up on my messages." She replied. "Stuff."

"Why don't you take the car today? You could drop me off and come back later when I'm done," he said.

Jessica thought about that for about a second, before answering, "Good idea. I'm desperate for more warm clothes." She pulled on her boots, giving them each a stomp to make sure her foot was comfortable, and reached for her jacket. Sparky danced at her feet, knowing they were going out. She wrapped him in his jacket, clipped on his leash, then picked up her purse, hat, and warm gloves. "All set."

Mike shook his head, "I've never seen anyone who can be ready to go so quickly."

Corked

She turned her blue eyes on him, "When you hang around with my dad, it's necessary. Anything more than ten minutes and he'll leave you behind."

"Are you one of them girls?" Mike asked, holding the door open for her.

"One of what girls?" She tugged lightly on Sparky's lead. "Let's go, bud."

"My favorite Lee Brice song," he said, as they entered the elevator. Pretending to sing into a microphone Mike belted out the few words he could remember, "... are you one of them girls, who likes to act all quiet. Sexy, not even tryin'. Yeah, you know I ain't lyin', damn right, you're one of them girls ..."

Laughing at his tuneless singing, they stepped out into the lobby and collided with the same woman they had met the day before. "Sorry, sorry. We weren't paying attention," Jessica apologized.

"No problem," the woman backed up a step. "I'd offer to shake your hand, but I'm told we aren't supposed to do that until the pandemic is under control," she said, then added, "We didn't introduce ourselves the other day, I'm Louise Newcomb. My husband and I are staying here for a few weeks. Perhaps we can get together for a drink some evening."

"A drink would be great, Louise. I'm Jessica Sanderson and this is Sparky," she pointed down,

162

"and our lead vocalist is Mike Lyons," she aimed a finger in Mike's direction.

"Pleased to meet you. What brings you to Penticton?" Louise asked.

"I'm a winery consultant," he replied, "Jessica is looking for work, and Sparky, well, he's our boss."

"There certainly are a lot of wineries in the valley, many that could use a good winemaker," Louise said, then added, "but, would it be rude to suggest you don't give up your day job for a singing career?"

"Jessica has already strongly recommended the same course of action," Mike agreed.

Sharing a laugh, they went in opposite directions — Louise into the elevator while Jessica, Mike and Sparky headed to the parking lot.

As the elevator doors closed, Louise's eyes followed Mike's retreating back. She thought she heard the woman, Jessica, say something about a murder.

"I wonder how the murder investigation is going?" Jessica speculated.

"Are you expecting the police to update you with their progress?" Mike opened the passenger-side door. "Are you driving?" he asked, looking at her for confirmation.

"Yep, I'm driving, and no, I don't expect the police to keep me informed, but I'm curious," she gave him a sly look. "I just don't want them to know how curious I am."

"Why?" He dropped into the seat and closed the door.

"If they think I am snooping around they won't be pleased with my interference." She opened the rear door and unclipped Sparky's leash from his harness.

"Well, here's a novel thought: Why don't you let them do their job and stay out of trouble?"

"I could, but where's the fun in that?" She motioned to the back seat. "Hop in, bud! We're taking Mike to work."

"Someone has to earn money to buy food for you, Sparkinator," Mike said to Sparky as he walked between the seats, spreading a wet mess of sand and snow on the console and sat down.

"Speaking of work, I know it's your first day but if you get the chance can you see if there is anything for me?"

"Yep, I just have to find an opportunity to ask Ellen Taylor."

"Maybe she won't be at work today. After all, her boss was murdered yesterday."

"Or the night before. I overheard Smith and her subordinate Jones when they were discussing the possible time of death."

"That's true; we were sent away before the coroner arrived so we don't know exactly when Quartermain died," Jessica hit the start button and checked over both shoulders, before backing up, "I wonder if Ellen will get promoted to general manager?"

"You are full of questions today. I don't know what her work experience is, and I imagine she'll be at work because someone has to take charge," Mike said.

"No one mentioned anything about closing it for a period of mourning," Jessica said, "but maybe they just forgot to let you know."

"A winery is basically a farm, with a manufacturing component. They are difficult to shut down," Mike replied. "We'll see what's happening when we get there."

"Yep," Jessica said, her attention drifting to another thought. "I sure hope the weather warms up soon. I'm already damn tired of being cold."

"Me too, although I'd like to try ice-fishing sometime," Mike said.

"Ice-fishing, now there's a sport that I'll never understand," Jessica said. "You don't have to fish for ice, you can make it in the freezer. I've got a really good recipe for homemade ice."

Mike laughed. It was just one more thing he loved about Jessica; her zany humor matched his.

Suddenly Jessica powered down the two back windows. "Dear god, Sparky, that's disgusting," she said. She felt the frosty wind whip through the vehicle as Mike lowered his window too.

"How do you know it was Sparky?" he asked innocently.

Chapter 24

RCMP detachment

Smith kicked her feet up, resting her boots on the corner of her desk and leaned back in the chair to get a good look at the murder board. "Not much information," she said.

"Give it time, it's only been thirty-six hours or so," Jones replied.

"Yes, but according to the television shows, we have to solve this in under forty-eight hours or we'll never figure it out," she dropped her feet, and swung them under the desk. "Let's split up that list of names, check for alibis, and do all of that other important stuff the police investigators do."

Jones grinned and held his hand out. "Give me half."

She pulled out the staple and separated the pages into two piles. She tapped her pile. "We should check the directors first; they are highlighted on the list. They have the most to lose with Quartermain's financial shenanigans."

Corked

"Love, lust, or loot — the three most common causes of murder," Jones said, skimming his finger down the list of names.

"Nope, profit, passion, and power," Smith said. "Power is a big one, especially for men."

"Semantics," Jones argued. "Let's take three each and check their alibis, then we can go back and question the others."

"Good idea. I'll start with the chairman. With a half a million tied up in a potentially worthless investment, he's my odds-on favorite."

"I wouldn't bet against that."

"You want a coffee?" Smith asked, getting to her feet and patting her pockets in search of change for the vending machine.

"Tastes like hot battery acid; I'll pass."

"How do you know what hot battery acid tastes like?"

"Just guessing."

"It's what's available, unless you want to do a Starbucks run?" She pocketed the coins then held out a twenty-dollar bill, "I'll pay."

Jones turned his phone over and checked the time. "Sure, why not. Maybe you'll have solved the murder by the time I get back." He snatched the money from her fingers and stuffed it into his pocket.

"Starbucks is only five minutes each way."

"Ah, but don't forget I have to stand in line, order, wait for the order, add sugar, stir, then apply the lids and the extra cardboard insulator-thingy so that you don't burn your delicate hands," he said, twirling the car keys on his finger. "It all adds up."

"Flirting with the baristas takes more time than all of the rest."

"Community policing relations."

"Does Meaghan agree with your community-minded flirting?"

"I'm all talk, and no action. She trusts me." He pushed the door open and walked out.

Smith picked up the phone handset, "All right, Mr. Douglas, let's see what you have to say for yourself today." She punched in his cell phone number.

"Your coffee ma'am," Jones said, putting the take-out container on Smith's desk.

She checked the time. "Impressive, thirty minutes of community policing. Is my coffee even still warm?"

Corked

"You can always nuke it if it's not hot enough."

Smith took a cautious sip. Starbucks coffee could go either way — so hot it would scald the roof of your mouth, or not nearly hot enough. "Nope, it's fine, thanks," and then she sucked in a big mouthful.

"You're welcome," Jones took off his heavy black jacket, and hung it over the back of a nearby chair, sat down and popped the lid on his coffee. "Did you solve the case yet?"

She chinned in the direction of the whiteboard, "I got Douglas's alibi nailed down. He was staying at a bed and breakfast. The owners said they stayed up to chat and share a nightcap with him before going to bed around one in the morning."

"And he didn't go out afterwards?"

"They are quite confident he didn't. They say they would have heard the gates open if he left the property."

Smith took another long pull of the coffee. It was her third cup of the day counting the two she made at home before heading into work. A murder investigation meant long hours and by the time she knocked off for the night, she might be on cup number seven or eight. She couldn't afford to always buy the good stuff, like Starbucks, and by the end of her shift she would resort to drinking the liquid from the vending machine, inappropriately labeled coffee.

"Okay, one down and forty-nine more to go, but when we add the cellar master Ben Whitaker, plus Jessica Sanderson and Mike Lyons to the suspect list," Jones said, "then we have fifty-two more alibis to check.

"I'll leave Ben Whitaker on the list for now. He works at the winery which gives him the opportunity, but I haven't discovered any motive yet, and his girlfriend Suzanne Johnson confirmed his alibi," Smith said between sips of coffee. "I also don't think Sanderson and Lyons are involved, but I haven't discounted them entirely. They were on the scene when we arrived, but again no motive that I can see."

"Did you get a hold of your retired buddy, Adair?"

"Yes, I did, and he knows quite a bit about Jessica Sanderson and her dog," Smith set her cup on the desk and leaned her forearms on her desk, shoulders hunched forward. "He sent me the links to several fascinating news articles about her."

Jones motioned with his fingers. "Give me the Coles Notes' version," he said.

"She's a well-known amateur detective who has had considerable success solving murders, and who has also become a general pain in the ass to the Mexican local and state police detectives," Smith replied.

"Hmm!" Jones thought about that for a second or two before replying, "I think we should arrest her, force a confession, and wrap this up today."

"Well, according to Adair, Ms. Sanderson will solve the case for us," Smith tipped her cup back and emptied it, then crumpled the cup and dropped in the trash container beside her desk.

"That disappeared quickly," Jones remarked, his interest in the story of Jessica Sanderson momentarily forgotten.

"I like to drink it while it's still hot." She opened her bottom desk drawer to check that her large bottle of antacids was still stashed there. She didn't need one now, but probably would later in the day. Picking up the bottle, she looked at Jones. "Someone has been snacking on my Rolaids. Was that you?"

"Nope, I don't touch that stuff."

"Well," she shook the partially full container, "being as I am a brilliant murder investigator, I deduce we must have mice with the ability to open bottles."

"Yep, that seems reasonable," he agreed. "By the way, if Jessica Sanderson solves our case, I will personally buy her a grande latte as a thank you."

Smith held out her hand. "Speaking of coffee, I'm sure I have some change coming from that twenty I handed you."

Jones reached in his front pocket and dug out an assortment of coins then stacked them like casino chips in front of Smith.

She poked the pile, knocking it over and raised an eyebrow. "That's it? That's my change?"

"I tipped the barista."

"How very generous of you."

Chapter 25

No Regrets Winery

Jessica pulled her pink woolen hat down over her ears, and zipped her navy jacket to her chin. Being inside the building wasn't much warmer than working in the vineyard. Today was her first day as a cellar-rat. Mike had asked Ellen Taylor if there was any casual work for her, and Ellen said she could start the next day.

She was the assistant to the assistant, the in-charge-of-nothing helper, but she had a job and she was working near, if not with, Mike.

Her first task had been to sweep the barrel room and put away the decorations left over from the recent shareholders' dinner. She was happy to be working physically rather than stuck behind a desk moving paper around; it meant she could eat whatever she wanted and didn't have to worry about gaining weight. The few days of hanging around the hotel suite waiting for Mike to finish work had already made her jeans feel snugger.

She heard footsteps, looked up and caught the smirk on Ben Whitaker's face. Instinctively her eyes dropped to check his hands; they were hidden behind his back.

"Catch!" Whitaker shouted as he and his assistant simultaneously tossed something in her direction. She stepped aside. The long, sinewy objects twisted in the air, then hit the floor, and quickly squirmed under the worktable.

"Beautiful," she said, squatting down to get a better look.

"What!" Whitaker shouted.

"They're bull snakes, right?" She looked him right in the eye, daring him to contradict her. The little dickhead thought he could frighten her by tossing a couple of snakes at her. Her two older brothers, Matt and Jake, had cured her at an early age of shrieking in fear, pretend or otherwise. Her brothers were her best friends, but at times when they were younger, their pranks were a gigantic pain in the arse. The best defense was calm acceptance of whatever deviltry they had planned.

"Well, yeah, they're bull snakes," Ben stammered, "but, how did you know? They could have been rattlesnakes." He was peeved at her response.

"Oval head, not triangular-shaped," she said. Her friendly smile masked her disapproval of their mistreatment of the creatures.

Corked

The snakes had unwittingly given her another clue to their identity as they sailed toward her. She hadn't heard the distinctive dry rattle sound of an agitated viper, and as reckless as they appeared to be, she couldn't visualize the two men casually hiding rattlesnakes behind their backs. She had instinctively decided they were harmless, and fortunately she was right.

She removed her glove and reached to gently pick up the closest one. The snake was as long as her outstretched arms, so about six feet or two meters. The dark and light pattern on its skin was remarkably similar to the marking on a rattlesnake.

"Bull snakes can easily be mistaken for rattlesnakes," she said, watching the snake contentedly wind itself around her arm and rest its large head on her warm palm. She removed the other glove and gently touched the dry cool skin of the creature. The reptile felt skinny from its winter hibernation.

She cooed to it, "Did you come out of hibernation too early, sweetie?"

"No, we pulled them out of the den," Ben said.

"That's mean," Jessica retorted. "It's too soon for snakes to be active."

"It was just a damn joke," he snapped back.

"Let's put these beauties back in their nice warm pit where they can snuggle with their buddies. You can take the other one," she said moving aside so that he could reach the snake. Jessica's lips twitched when she saw the other prankster slink off behind the barrels. *You'll have to try harder than that to scare me.*

Coming out of the vineyard Mike walked to the paved parking area and knocked the mud off of his boots, then headed toward the building. The snow had melted, creating a glutinous muck that stuck to everything, like poop on a baby's behind. A chilly north wind whipped down the valley, rattling the dormant grape vines and made the mildly pleasant day feel downright nippy. He shivered, stuffed his gloves in his pockets, opened the door, and shouted, "Hey Ben, are you in here?"

"Here," Whitaker answered, curtly.

"Boy, it's damn chilly out there, a heck of a lot colder than Mexico," Mike said, moving toward Ben's voice. "What're you up to?"

"Transferring the Chardonnay, for bottling," he replied without taking his eyes off the pump.

"Good, I was going to suggest that," Mike said. He caught a fleeting expression on Ben's face, a cross between disdain and ridicule. He had been expecting it. Almost every contract started off with the regular employees resenting his suggestions, but in time he was usually able to win them over. He was seldom impatient, or critical, just calm and steady, with a willingness to compliment others and laugh at himself.

"Have you seen Jessica around?" Mike asked.

"She's washing down the crush pad," Whitaker responded, still not making eye contact.

"Okay, thanks. I'll be back in a minute or two," Mike said, walking toward the back door.

"You do that, big man," Whitaker mumbled to his retreating back.

"Hey, Jess, how are you doing?" Mike stepped over the hose that stretched across the concrete pad, he hugged her and gave her a gentle kiss.

"Good. I'm a bit cold, especially my feet, but it's fine as long as I keep moving." She closed the nozzle on the hose shutting off the water. "At least it's a bit warmer today."

"True, except the wind-chill makes it feel colder. What have you been doing besides washing down the crush pad?" He briskly rubbed his hands up and down her arms, warming her.

"Oh, you know, bit of this and that, cleaning up and snake wrangling."

"Snake wrangling?" he guffawed. "What's that about?"

She cocked her head and gave him one of her mischievous, I've-got-this smiles. "Ben and the other guy, I can't remember his name, tried to frighten the new girl today."

"The other guy's name is Chris Berry," Mike said with a hint of concern in his voice. "What did they do?"

"Right, Chris," she said as she snapped her fingers, "that's the little turd's name. They tossed a couple of big bull snakes at me, thinking I was going to run outside shrieking like a little kid."

"Bull snakes, I've heard they'll bite when they are pissed off," he stated. Judging by the wicked grin on Jessica's face, she had maintained the upper hand, but he was annoyed because the guys had been irresponsible. "Are you okay?"

"I'm fine, and don't make a fuss about it. They were just testing me. I didn't react to their juvenile joke, instead I picked up one of the snakes and had a nice chat with it," she explained.

"Now that is funny," he said, then added, "Where did the snakes go?" He looked down at his feet, as if he was expecting an invasion of large, slithery reptiles.

Corked

"I told Ben we had to put them back where they found them. Snakes need warmer weather."

"All right then, that explains his grumpy response when I talked to him." Mike winked at her.

"Yeah, I kind of ruined their fun and they weren't pleased." Her eyes shone with mischief.

"He seemed annoyed, that's for sure."

"I was hoping to quiz him about company gossip in hopes of working out who killed Quartermain, so now, I guess I'll have to play nice and make a fresh pot of coffee and take him one."

Chapter 26

No Regrets Winery

"Coffee?" Jessica asked. She held two cups, one in each hand. "It's fresh," she set the cups on the nearest flat surface, and dug in her pocket. "Here's sugar, a few of those little creamer capsules, and ta-da, a spoon," she said whipping it out with a flourish.

"Thanks, I appreciate it." Ben straightened, stretched and rolled his shoulders, then reached for one of the cups. "Hey, no hard feelings about earlier, eh? We were just joking around."

"No worries, I have two older brothers so I'm used to stuff like that." She looked at Chris Berry, who was still avoiding eye contact. "Do you want a coffee, Chris?"

"Yeah, great, thanks," he said, then picked up the second cup, stirred in a bit of sugar and cream. "Thanks again." Head down, he moved a few feet away and leaned against a stack of barrels.

"So, you aren't going to complain to Ellen, or Mr. Douglas?" Ben asked, his eyes watchful over the rim of his coffee cup.

Jessica scoffed at his question, "Good grief, no. Just leave those poor snakes alone and we're fine."

Chris visibly relaxed and finally met her eyes. "How do you know so much about snakes," he asked.

"I worked as a waitress in Penticton for one summer, plus I helped out in a peach orchard at harvest time. I had encounters with snakes of all types," she said, *including the human variety.* "They really are fascinating."

"Right," Chris said, with heavy skepticism, "fascinating."

"In other words, the only reason you picked up that snake was to torment the new girl?" Jessica turned the full wattage of her smile on Chris and watched him blush.

He scuffed his work boot on the concrete and tossed a glance to Ben, then his lips twisted with an embarrassed smile, "Yeah," he agreed.

"As I said, I grew up with two brothers who took great pleasure in tormenting me, so let's just forget about this and start over. Deal?" Jessica offered her hand for him to shake, then pulled it back. "Sorry, I forgot, no shaking hands."

"Deal," Chris agreed, "and we don't need to shake on it."

"How long have you guys worked here?" Jessica said, boosting herself onto a barrel, settling in for a longer chat.

Chris answered, "Six months for me. Ben, what are you, almost a year now?"

"A year in April."

"Do you like working here?" she asked.

"It's okay," Chris said. "I'm just a cellar-rat, doing the manual labor like you."

Ben heard the whine of the pump change pitch, meaning the tank was empty and the pump was about to run dry. He put his cup down, and closed the valve to prevent the tank from draining back through the pump then flicked off the power.

Ben didn't answer her question about if he liked working as the cellar master, so she tried another one. "I've never bottled before. Can I help?" she asked.

"Sure, we have the mobile bottling line booked for tomorrow morning, bright and early. Be here by eight," Ben said. He tipped his cup, finished the coffee, then set the cup down.

"I don't understand. Doesn't the winery have their own equipment?"

Corked

"Nope, we rent it," Ben answered. "The equipment is too expensive for most small to medium-sized companies to have their own, so a couple of companies have sprung up in the valley."

Chris added, "Dress warmly, bring a lunch and something to drink if you don't want to guzzle coffee all day. We work until we've emptied the tanks."

"Okay, sounds good." Watching Ben, Jessica casually asked, "What was Kingsley Quartermain like to work for?"

Ben busied himself with disconnecting the pump from the transfer hoses. Chris pulled a garden hose over and started rinsing out the equipment. "He was okay as a boss," Ben finally replied.

"I heard he had a temper," Jessica lied. She hadn't heard anything about Kingsley good or bad — she was fishing for information.

"Nah, not really. As long as you did your job, he left you alone," Ben answered, then said to Chris, "I'm going to transfer the rest of the Pinot Blanc," he said. "We have an order for another pallet."

"Sure."

Jessica caught the side-eye action between the two men and couldn't help wondering what that was all about. Were they lying about Quartermain

184

having a bad temper? Or were they hiding something, like theft of a few bottles of wine? Whatever was going on, they obviously weren't in the mood to dish the dirt.

"Okay, my break is over. I'll get back to working on that list of jobs you gave me this morning." Jessica hopped off the barrel and dusted off the back of her jeans. She picked up the empty coffee cups, "Catch you, later."

"Yep, thanks again for the coffee, Jessica," Chris said.

"What are you doing, faking more Pinot Blanc?" Chris hissed at Ben once Jessica was out of sight.

"Chill out. Our sales rep sold another pallet before I could tell him not to, not that he'd listen to me anyway," Ben griped. "This is the last one. Besides no one knows what's going on except you and me." He roughly shoved the transfer pump toward a second tank of the soon to be relabeled Chardonnay.

"And Ellen. She's the general manager now."

"Temporary general manager. She a scared little mouse; she won't do anything."

"I'm not happy doing this."

185

"I don't give a damn if you aren't happy, Chris," Ben sneered. "We aren't going to blow off the sale. The business is in deep financial shit with the stuff that Quartermain pulled."

"Are we still going to get paid?"

"Sure, as long as we keep supplying product and our sales rep keeps selling it, we're fine." Ben roughly slammed the hose couplings into place.

Chris flinched at the sound of the metal fastener being pummelled into place. "What's the deal with you and Jessica? You seem kind of hostile toward her."

"She's the girlfriend of that big shot consultant that Quartermain hired to oversee my work," Ben retorted.

"He seems like a decent guy."

"Oh sure, big smiles. Do this, Ben. Do that, Ben. As if I can't find my own ass with my two hands." He checked the hose connections then flipped the switch. "I think he's looking for any opportunity to criticize me or maybe get me fired."

"Cut the guy a break. He was hired to win medals for the wine. Maybe we can learn from him."

"Well, you just go ahead and do that. I've got experience and training, and I sure as hell don't need some part-time winemaker coming in here to tell me how to do my job."

"Did you have an argument with Quartermain about hiring Mike Lyons?"

Ben stopped what he was doing, and squared his frame, "What the hell are you implying?" He snarled.

Chris's eyes dropped to the large crescent wrench being strangled by Ben's hand. "Nothing."

Chapter 27

Okanagan

"What are you going to do with Sparky today?" Mike asked as he finished his coffee, then rinsed out the cup and tipped it over on the drain board. "I hate to leave him on his own again."

"Me too, so I asked Ellen yesterday if it would be okay if he was at the winery with us, and she said it was fine as long as he didn't get in the way."

"That's great," Mike sat and pulled on his warm boots, "I know a lot of vineyards have dogs on the premises, part pets, part guard dogs, and part rodent control."

"Yep. I figured that out when I spotted the BC humane society's fundraising calendar in the gift shop," she said. "It has dozens of photos of the winery dogs of BC. They are so stinking cute I want to visit all of the properties just to meet all of the pooches."

Mike looked up. "Not much socializing going on these days. Everyone is busy bottling their whites or pruning the vines in preparation for the growing season, and then we have the challenges of the coronavirus restrictions."

"I know, but some day things will normalize, and then we can go touring, taste a bunch of fabulous wines and eat delicious meals in the bistros."

"Sounds good, but now we have to get a move on, or we'll be late," he playfully swatted her with his gloves.

Thirty minutes later Jessica turned the Sonata into the staff parking area at *No Regrets Winery*, and spotted a large Kenworth truck with a long trailer parked close to the tall wooden doors. "I guess that's the mobile line that Ben was talking about."

"Yep, they can probably do two thousand cases in a day with that setup."

"That's a lot of wine," she said. "Are you working with us today?"

"It's a big job and usually everyone pitches in with bottling, but I'll leave that up to Ben. He can tell me what he needs help with."

"A little fence mending?"

"Exactly."

Corked

Mike swung his legs out of the passenger's side, then waited for Jessica and Sparky before heading toward the trailer unit.

"Hey, Jessica, how are you?" Chris Berry asked, with a wide smile. He bent down and offered his hand to Sparky to smell. "Who's this little guy?"

Oh, now you are my new best friend. "I'm good, Chris. This is Sparky," she patted her leg, signaling him to stay close. "Ellen said it was okay to bring him as long as he doesn't get in the way," she said. "What can I help with?"

Ben piped up, "Start with Sharon, putting the full bottles into the cases."

Chris waved at a tall woman with shoulder-length auburn hair. "Hey, Sharon, this is Jessica. She's going to work with you."

"Another redhead," Jessica mumbled.

"What?" Chris asked.

"Nothing, it's just I have met a lot of redheads recently and was wondering if it was something in the water," Jessica said.

Chris turned a puzzled expression her way He obviously had no idea what she was going on about.

"Hi, Jessica, I'm Sharon Hickey. Welcome to our crazy world," she said.

"Hi, pleased to meet you. Can you show me what I'm supposed to be doing?"

"Sure," Sharon said, "stand here. Once the line gets going, I'll take six bottles and put them in a case, then the case will move to your position, and you add six bottles. Make sure you check the labels. They need to be straight, even, and securely glued."

"How do I check the labels?"

"Pick up the bottle, quickly scan it, and put it in the case. If you aren't happy with the label set it aside. As soon as we have a minute of downtime we go back and recheck the labels, and if necessary, remove and reapply another one."

"Sounds easy," Jessica said.

Sharon's laugh was a rich friendly chuckle, "It is until you have been doing it non-stop for a few hours, and your feet feel like two blocks of ice, and your hands are stiff. We try to change jobs every hour or two just to keep warm."

Mike joined the group. "Can I help?"

"You can stack the full cases on the pallet," Ben answered, curtly. "Everyone ready?"

"All set," Sharon answered and nodded at Jessica.

Jessica pointed to a sheltered spot near the bottling line, "Lay down, Sparky, and stay out of the way." She turned to watch as the machine lined

Corked

up the new bottles, inverted them, sprayed inside
to remove dust, and righted them before moving
them into the filling position. Once the bottles were
filled the machine applied the screw cap and a
plastic seal. "That's amazing."

"Yes, we can package fifty-six cases in
fifteen minutes. It's a lot quicker than the old
method of filling one bottle at a time." Sharon said,
"Here we go," as the first bottles arrived at her
workstation.

Jessica frantically grabbed the arriving
bottles, checked labels and stuffed six in a case,
only to find the next case was already pushing to
get past. "Holy hell, this thing is fast."

The next hour flew past in a blur of repetitive
movements, as case after case arrived in front of
her, she found herself breathing harder and
perspiring despite the wintery temperature.

"Change," Ben yelled as he paused the
bottling line. "Rotate one position. Hustle folks,
let's go!"

Another hour and every muscle in Jessica's
body ached with the pain of the unfamiliar work.
Dear god, I'm going to be stiff tomorrow. She
flicked a quick glance at Sparky — he was napping.
Smart dog.

"Fifteen-minute break after this case is
done," Ben shouted.

Corked

The line stopped moving. Jessica leaned against the side of the trailer, breathing deeply. "You okay, Jess?" Mike asked.

"Yep, I'm good. Tomorrow will be a different story though. Everything hurts," she replied. "But right now, I need a pee and a big drink of water."

By late morning, Jessica had become accustomed to the rapid pace and was able to start a conversation with Sharon. "How long have you been doing this?"

"I usually work in the wine shop at Ruby Blues on the Naramata Bench, but I frequently get asked to help out with bottling at other properties."

"It's a good exercise program."

"Not as rigorous as my dragon boat racing," Sharon countered.

"Dragon boat racing, that would be exciting."

"It is. I'm part of the Survivorship team. We're all breast cancer survivors."

"I'm impressed," Jessica said, and meant it. Sharon was a breast cancer survivor and a dragon boat paddler — that was remarkable.

Continuing to work, they chatted about the international racing events that Sharon had participated in, then the weather, and how the days were finally getting longer but neither one liked to drive at night because of the deer and other animals on the roads. "I nearly had an accident driving home the other night," Sharon said.

"What happened?" Jessica asked.

"I was out for dinner at a friend's house and I was driving back quite late when a dark-colored SUV barreled out of this road and nearly t-boned my car," Sharon said.

"This road?" Jessica asked. "It's just a country lane for heaven's sake, and no need to speed. Was the driver drunk?"

"I don't know, but certainly driving too fast on the snow-covered road."

"Maybe he swerved to avoid the wild sheep."

"I didn't see any, but then I was concentrating on avoiding an accident."

Jessica thought for a minute, then her curiosity got the better of her. "What night was that?"

"Saturday night, the 14th."

Her *snoopervisor* antenna, as Mike called it, quivered. "Interesting," she muttered to herself, "that's the same night that Kingsley Quartermain was murdered."

"Pardon?" Sharon asked, over the roar of the machinery.

"Oh, nothing. I'm just making a mental list of groceries to buy on the way home tonight," Jessica fibbed.

Awhile later as the winter sun dipped below the mountains, Ben called a stop. "That's the Chardonnay done — let's clean up," he said. "Tomorrow we'll do the Pinot Blanc, and the Gewürztraminer."

Again, Jessica caught a heated scowl that Chris lobbed at Ben. *What's that about?* She glanced at Mike to see if he had noticed, but he was crouched down talking to Sparky and not watching the others.

Jessica, Mike and Sparky climbed into their rental car, and headed back to the hotel. Mike had one hand on the steering wheel, the other one held Jessica's hand. "Long day today?" he asked, tipping a smile at her.

"God, yes," she agreed, "I'm going to be sore tomorrow." She rested her head against the window.

"I know what you mean. Ben made sure that I spent the entire day lifting the full cases onto the pallet," Mike said. "I've rediscovered a whole lot of muscles that I had forgotten about."

"Maybe he felt sorry for the delicate little ladies, and wanted the big strong guy to do the heavy work."

"Maybe, or maybe he wanted to assert his authority over the interloper — me."

"Could be," Jessica said, "by the way, did you notice the interaction between Chris and Ben?"

"When?"

"Right at the end of the day when Ben was talking about bottling tomorrow."

"No," Mike said, shaking his head, "I didn't."

Jessica sighed, shifted in her seat and chewed her bottom lip. "Maybe I am imagining it but that's twice I've noticed several unhappy looks from Chris when Ben talks about the wine. Something is really bothering him."

"I trust your instincts, Jess," Mike said, signaling to turn north onto Highway 97. "I'll poke around a bit and see if I can figure out what's going on."

"Be careful with your snooping," she said as she squeezed his hand. "We still don't know who killed Quartermain."

"Good point. Both guys are fit enough that they could have done it," Mike said.

"Bashed on the head, twice, then dragged to the forklift, then a rope tied around his neck and the forks raised until his feet were off the ground," Jessica stated. "Even I could have killed him that way, but I have an alibi. We were at the airport when he died."

Mike shot her a startled look. "You've really been thinking about this."

"You know me. The Assassin of Isla Mujeres," she said.

"I'll make sure I stay on your good side."

She patted his hand. "That's an excellent idea."

Chapter 28

RCMP Detachment

Smith made a note on her list and checked off another potential suspect: shareholder Frank Anderson had an alibi, his wife.

Spousal alibis weren't always truthful, but for the moment she was trying to whittle down the list to something more manageable than the entire group of shareholders and employees. The board of directors, her odds-on favorites, had been checked first but every one had a reasonably good alibi. Still, that didn't guarantee that all the personal references were rock solid.

She had been able to scoop another investigator to help them, and they should be able to finish the preliminary checks today. She lifted her head, and looked at Jones. "Ethan, how're you doing on your list?"

"I just finished. Do you need help with yours?"

"Sure, I have four left." She scribbled two names and phone numbers on a bit of paper and handed it to him. She noticed Constable Natalie

Garcha put down the phone and stretch her arms overhead. "Nat," she said, "how about you? Have you finished?"

"Yes, that was my last one," Natalie picked up her coffee cup, peered into it, then tossed the empty container into the bin under her desk. "Three didn't go to the event at the winery because of prior commitments. The rest have spousal alibis," she said as she fluttered her hand in an indecisive motion.

"I've got the same situation," Jones interjected. "Almost all of the investors were at the event as couples and staying overnight in local hotels, so we know where they say they were, but we don't know that they actually were in their rooms at the time of the murder."

Smith stood and wandered over to stand in front of the whiteboard. "Damn little to go on so far," she said as she looked at her co-workers. "Either of you have any brilliant, new ideas?"

"I might be more inspired after another cup of coffee," Jones cheekily waggled his eyebrows at Smith.

"I'll go," Natalie spoke up, "I need some fresh air." She loosened her thick black hair from the tight bun at the back of her head, vigorously scrubbed her fingers over her scalp, then rewrapped and secured her hair again.

Watching her, Jones asked, "I've seen you do that a few times today, Nat. Why?"

Natalie turned her chocolate brown eyes on him, and winked. "Just to get your motor running, big boy." It was common knowledge that even though Jones liked to look at pretty women, he was devoted to his wife Meaghan, and he didn't stray. Ever. Natalie liked that about Jones, and felt comfortable with a bit of harmless flirting.

"Nice."

She stood, pulled on her jacket, and picked up the keys to her vehicle. "My hair is heavy and it pulls on my scalp. It helps to loosen it once in awhile," she said, "and get the blood flowing again."

"So, you're restarting your brain?"

She popped her middle finger up, "You can buy the coffee for that comment."

Jones chuckled good-naturedly and tossed Natalie a twenty-dollar bill. "Grande latte for me."

Natalie scooped up the money. "And what can I get you, Caitlin?"

Smith turned from scrutinizing the board. "A guilty perp would be nice — otherwise I'll take a grande latte, too, thanks."

Chapter 29

No Regrets Winery

"Good morning, Ben," Mike said. "All ready for today?"

Ben Whitaker stopped abruptly, nearly tripping over his own feet, when he saw who was waiting for him.

"What are you doing here so early?" Ben snapped. "I didn't see your car in the parking lot."

"It's over on the side of the building, out of the way," Mike gestured toward the south side of the building. He had deliberately parked it where it couldn't easily be seen from the staff parking area, "I'm early because I wanted to speak privately with you."

"Ooooh, that sounds really serious," Ben taunted.

Mike didn't react, he merely replied, "We won't be bottling any Pinot Blanc today. We'll finish bottling the Chardonnay."

"What are you talking about? We did all of the Chardonnay yesterday," Ben bluffed.

201

"I know the difference between the two varietals," Mike countered, holding up a small tasting glass. "I sampled all of the white wines in the cellar this morning, before I had coffee or anything to eat, just to be sure my palate and taste buds were clean and fresh." Mike set the glass down, and folded his arms across his chest. "There isn't any Pinot Blanc in any of the tanks. Furthermore, there aren't any records of Pinot Blanc grapes being grown in any of our vineyards, or purchased from our contract grape growers."

Ben silently glared at Mike.

"What are you playing at, Ben? Why mislabel the Chardonnay as Pinot Blanc?"

"It's none of your damn business."

"On the contrary, while I am under contract everything that happens in this cellar is my business," Mike refuted. "What's your game?"

"I must have made a mistake," he mumbled.

"Incorrectly identifying a wine is a very serious mistake for a cellar master. But what concerns me more is the labels and the bar code for a product that we don't make. That could be grounds for dismissal," Mike said, hoping to provoke a reaction.

"Listen, you interfering bastard," Ben shouted, "it was Quartermain who organized the labels and the barcode. He's the one who told me to bottle a full pallet, fifty-six cases of Pinot Blanc, and to ship it to Vancouver."

"He's dead, Ben," Mike said, "and he's been dead for what, nine or ten days now. Exactly how did he tell you to make the switch?"

"It happened back in February. The sales rep sold the wrong type of wine, and Quartermain didn't want to lose the sale," Ben sputtered. "It wasn't my decision!"

"Again, he's dead. You were going to do another fifty-six cases and ship them to our warehouse in Vancouver. That," Mike said and paused for emphasis, "is squarely on you."

"Same story: stupid sales rep, and we needed the sale."

"This illegal crap stops now," Mike said putting a bit of heat in his voice.

"Screw you! I quit!" Ben yelled, then stomped out of the building.

Mike straightened up and turned around, "Did you hear all of that?" he asked.

"Yes, and I recorded it on my phone," Jessica said, moving out from behind the tank, "just in case he tries to put the blame on you."

The corners of Mike's eyes crinkled, "You're really into this detective stuff."

Jessica tipped her head to one side, "Your first clue should have been the video recording sunglasses I wore the day we met."

"I remember! They were a joke gift from Diego and they accidently helped solve the murder of the musician, Brandon Forbes."

"Exactly," Jessica agreed.

"Good morning, Mike, Jessica," Chris Berry called as he walked toward them. "I just saw Ben driving away. He looked angry. Is everything okay?"

"Morning, Chris," Mike answered, "Ben has tendered his resignation as of a few minutes ago."

"Ah hell, I shouldn't have said anything to you."

"You did the right thing, Chris," Mike said. "I really appreciate you being candid."

"Well, I was really uncomfortable with what he was doing, but I didn't know who to complain to. Besides, with Quartermain gone, I really thought it would stop," Chris said.

"Not to worry, let's get set up for bottling. The others will be here soon."

"Hey Mike?"

"Yeah?"

"Did you tell Ellen?"

"Yes, I told her I know all about the switching. She wasn't aware that he was planning to do it again."

"Am I going to be fired?"

"Nope. You were honest when I asked and we need you," Mike said, "so let's get to work."

Chapter 30

No Regrets Winery

"Lockdown!" Jessica exclaimed. "What the hell?"

Perched on a tall stool in the warehouse, Mike was checking the latest reports. "What's up?" he asked. He titled his gaze up from the papers to meet hers.

She read from her phone screen, "Doctor Bonnie Henry, the top doctor in BC has implemented a province-wide lockdown to prevent the spread of the coronavirus. Only essential businesses can remain open. The border between Canada and the USA is closed, and only emergency travel is allowed anywhere in the province."

"It's a good thing we left Mexico before the planes stopped flying," Mike said.

Jessica flicked a look at him. "Being confined to Mexico wouldn't have been a terrible thing. We have friends there, I can always find work at *Loco Lobo* or another restaurant, and we have a place to live, but more importantly — it's warm. March in

Mexico is a heck of a lot warmer than March in Canada."

Mike reached for her phone and read the article, then handed it back, "I could definitely be out of a job, again. And if tourism stops, then even if you were still on Isla, you wouldn't be working either but you would be warm."

"Damn it," Jessica flopped into a chair, "you really think they'll cancel your contract?"

"I can't expect to be paid if I can't work."

"This is awful, Mike."

"It certainly puts a kink in things, but there's no use getting stressed until we know more about our situation."

Scanning the list of businesses that were allowed to continue operating, Jessica recited part of the list, "... grocery stores, pharmacies, gas stations, and liquor stores. If the liquor stores can remain open, maybe the wineries will be okay as well."

"I wouldn't count on it," Mike said, "but they could probably sell existing product to the stores."

She huffed and continued reading, "Look at this, pawnbrokers are considered an essential service and are permitted to remain open. Since when are pawn-brokers a necessity?"

"If someone needs to cash in a family heirloom to buy food, I suppose that qualifies as important."

"Is there any way you can find out about your status?"

"I'll check with Ellen to see if she has heard anything," Mike said as he headed toward the stairway leading to the administration offices.

"Wait, I'm coming with you." Jessica scurried after him. "It affects me too, even though I am just a lowly warehouse worker not the big shot wine consultant."

"The lowly warehouse worker might be the one who still has a job. Your wages cost a lot less than this big shot wine consultant."

"Fricking hell, this year is turning out to be a bitch," she said as they walked into the upstairs office.

"Hi, Mike. Hi, Jess, what's up?" Ellen asked.

"Have you heard anything about the province-wide lockdown?" Jessica asked.

"No. What's a lockdown?"

"Everything — schools, churches, businesses, except essential services are closed until further notice," Jessica replied.

"When did that start?"

"Today. Only a few businesses can remain open. Everyone else has to shelter in place at home," Mike answered.

Jessica handed Ellen her phone with the article displayed on the screen.

Ellen rocked her head back, "That's serious. Shutting down so many businesses will cause economic havoc." She handed the phone back to Jessica. "I'll call Matthew Douglas, the chairman of the board, and find out what they want me to do."

"Mind if we wait here while you call?" Asked Mike.

"Sure," Ellen said, pointing at the two chairs in front of her desk, "have a seat. I'll see what he has to say." Her eyes focused on her desk, waiting for the call to be answered, "Hello, Mr. Douglas, this is Ellen."

Jessica and Mike could hear his voice, but couldn't make out the words when Douglas answered.

"Have you seen the news today?" Ellen asked and waited for Douglas to reply, then she briefly met Mike's eyes and shook her head. No, Douglas hadn't heard the news.

"Doctor Bonnie Henry, our provincial health officer, has instituted a shutdown of all non-essential businesses. The schools are not reopening after spring break. Travel is restricted to inside our own communities. She has reenforced the two meter/six feet social distancing and put a ban on group gatherings," Ellen said. Then as the torrent of angry sounds erupted, she held the phone away from her ear.

"What does that bloody woman think she is doing?" Douglas shouted. "She'll drive our business, and possibly the country, into bankruptcy with those ludicrous restrictions." His response was clearly heard by everyone in the room.

"I'm sorry, Mr. Douglas, it's not something we have any control over. Would you like to speak to the other directors, then get back to me with instructions?" Ellen asked.

"Yes."

By now Ellen knew that Douglas would not end the call politely, he would just hang up, so she wasn't surprised when once again she was listening to dead air. She put the phone back on its base, and looked at Mike and Jessica. "As you can tell, he's a bit unhappy about the information."

"I'm surprised he didn't already know," said Mike.

"His home is in Alberta, not BC. That government has had a different response to the crisis and he probably hadn't checked the national news yet."

"He was here when Quartermain died so I thought he lived in BC," Mike said.

"He visits frequently and was here for the spring shareholders' meeting when Kingsley died, but for the most part the board of directors didn't, until recently, have much to do with the day-to-day business of the winery," Ellen explained.

Mike nodded in understanding. He'd heard the gossip about Quartermain embezzling money from the company, and since his death the directors were more in evidence. In his opinion it was too little too late, but he was only a contract worker, not an investor. "Okay, what would you like Jessica and me to do?"

"Just keep working until I hear otherwise. We bottled some of the whites at the beginning of March just before you arrived, and then we finished the remainder the other day. As you know, the reds won't be ready for bottling until the fall."

Mike and Jessica waited in silence while Ellen organized her thoughts. "We need to prune the vines, repair the trellises and the irrigation system, and tidy the vineyard. And of course, keep control of the juices fermenting in the tanks; otherwise, the last year's vintage will be lost," Ellen said.

"I agree," Mike said, then added, "I'm curious, why aren't you being confirmed as the new general manager? You know the industry."

Corked

"I'm a woman," she said, stating the obvious. "The directors are bringing in a man to take over."

Chapter 31

FaceTime call

"*Hola seesta*, you're looking good," Jessica said when the call connected to Yasmin on Isla Mujeres.

"And you look cozy all bundled up in your turtleneck sweater and jeans. Are you enjoying the weather in Canada?" Yasmin asked. "I'm a little warm in my shorts and top," she teased, then tugged on the front of her blouse as if she was trying to cool down.

"Stop tormenting me," Jessica said. "It's only ten degrees Celsius here, or about fifty something in Fahrenheit."

"Brrr, that's too cold for my Mexican blood," Yasmin said. "How are you and Mike doing?"

"We're okay, but the government has closed all non-essential businesses. The wine shop and restaurant were already closed for the slow season and won't reopen until the lockdown is lifted. According to our boss we are allowed to work in the vineyards and to supervise the wine in the tanks."

213

"Does that mean you and Mike are still working?"

"For now. Who knows what will happen next?" Jessica said. "The lockdown has also cancelled our plans to drive to Vancouver and introduce Mike to my family."

"Woo hoo, meeting the family. Things must be getting serious."

"No, not really. We're still figuring out our relationship, but I really wanted to visit with Mom and Dad and my two dorky brothers. I haven't seen them since they came to Isla for your wedding a year ago."

"I remember and I wouldn't call your brothers dorky. More like hunky, seriously hunky," Yasmin said.

"You didn't live with them," Jessica retorted with a smile.

"How about Mike's family? Where do they live?"

"His mom and dad live in Kingston, Ontario. We can't visit them either," she said. "Flights have been cancelled indefinitely."

"Yeah, same here," Yasmin agreed. "Does Mike have any brothers or sisters?"

"No, he's an only child."

"I don't think I would want to be an only child," Yasmin said. "My parents would have too many expectations for me to live closer to them, and I don't want to move to Mérida. It's too hot in the summer."

"Except you and Carlos are trying to have a family and once the grandbabies start arriving you or they will be moving closer," Jessica rebutted.

"I think I'm safe. My sister Adriana and her husband Enrique live in Mérida. They keep my mom and dad occupied with their two boys."

"But your nephews are almost teenagers, and they won't have time for grandparents soon," Jessica teased. Yasmin adored her family, but Jessica had met her mother, Maria Victoria Guzman de Medina, a few years ago and knew she was a strong-willed person. If the formidable Victoria wanted the grandchildren to live nearby, she would relentlessly suggest, request, and assert that Yasmin and Carlos should move closer.

"Any news on the murder of that man at the winery?" Yasmin asked, changing the subject.

"Not really. The RCMP detectives have questioned everyone, some twice. Mike and I have been hauled over the coals too. But no one has been charged, as far as we know," Jessica said.

"Why are they questioning you?"

"Uh, well, we were here shortly after the body was discovered, and … I might have blabbed a bit too much about living in Mexico and about Sparky's abilities. The detective kept asking more questions —that just dug a deeper hole for me."

Yasmin sighed. "You just can't stay away from dead bodies."

"It's not my fault," Jessica replied. "So, how are things on the island?"

"We're shut down too. Only one person per family can be outside the house at any time. One person to fuel the family vehicle. One person to walk the dog or dogs. One person to shop for groceries, if you can find anything in the stores. The shelves are stripped bare as soon as they are restocked."

"So, I guess you have a toilet paper shortage too?"

"*Si, es muy loco*," Yasmin agreed, "and we have a meat shortage. What about you?"

"A panic-induced shortage of paper goods, eggs, butter, fresh vegetables, and meat. A few people went into the big stores and stacked their shopping carts with every single cut of meat they could lay their hands on, until someone posted a video on social media," Jessica said.

"Then what happened?"

"The backlash was instant and fierce. One couple publicly apologized and made a large cash donation to the local food bank."

"Serves them right for being greedy," Yasmin said, then added, "There's one funny thing that has happened recently. The supply of Nutella is now under lock and key at Chedraui stores."

"Why?" Jessica couldn't think why a commonly available nut-flavored breakfast spread would be so valuable. It was like locking up peanut butter.

Yasmin giggled. "It was being shoplifted by amorous couples wanting to relieve a bit of the lockdown boredom. Nutella is the hot new body spread."

"That's hilarious," Jessica said.

"It's the truth," Yasmin said.

Still chuckling, Jessica asked, "How are you and Carlos doing?"

"We're fine, but the construction of the new restaurant, *A Pirate's Delight*, has stopped, due to the lockdown," Yasmin said.

"Ha! You finally realized the name I suggested was the perfect choice."

"Yes, we did."

"Awesome," Jessica said, "but I'm sorry to hear about the construction delays. All that money that you've invested and no idea when you can open the restaurant."

"It's difficult, but we are grateful that we still have food on the table and a roof over our heads," Yasmin said. "Many islanders are having a really tough time a and a group of us are fundraising for a new charity to provide basic groceries."

"Mike and I'll contribute. Where do we send the money to?"

"If you are sure you can afford it, that would really be appreciated," Yasmin said. "It's a PayPal account."

"I'll do that as soon as we end this call, but honestly, Yassy, are you and Carlos okay?"

"Yes, we are. And I have been checking in with the others too. Diego and Pedro's fishing charter company has slowed down because of the health warnings, and incoming flights were cancelled but now with the enforced quarantine hardly anyone is working. Pedro and Maricruz have moved in together to save money. They are doing okay because they still have her Navy paycheck. It is difficult for everyone. Even the beaches are closed."

"The beaches? Why?"

"The government is worried about crowds, so everything is shut down. Homeowners can't even use the beach in front of their house."

"That's depressing. Living in paradise and trapped inside your house," Jessica said.

"And the Isla *policía* are stationed in the ferry terminals, on the Cancun side, checking IDs. If you aren't a resident you can't come to the island," she said, "and once you do get here you have to walk through a misting tunnel that sprays disinfectant all over you and your stuff."

"I wouldn't like that."

"But the oddest thing is the complete ban on alcohol on the island."

"What?"

"I know. The restaurants and bars are closed and the stores can't sell it," Yasmin said. "Some people were ordering alcohol from Amazon, but the authorities put a stop to that. No more alcohol deliveries to the island."

"But can't people just go to Cancun purchase booze?"

"Yes, at the few stores that are open, like Costco, but it gets confiscated at the ferry terminals."

"Ah jeez, in lockdown, no alcohol, and no beach time. That's awful. Let's talk about happier things," Jessica said. "Are you and Carlos pregnant yet?"

"Carlos isn't."

"Are you?"

"Maybe."

"Yassy," Jessica excitedly squealed, "you either are or you aren't … you can't be *maybe* pregnant."

"I'm on my way to the pharmacy for a pregnancy test kit as soon as we are finished catching up."

"Oh my god. I'm so excited."

"Slow down, *seesta*. I haven't done the test yet," Yasmin cautioned.

"Okay, okay. Deep breaths. But you have to call me the instant you know — one way or the other."

"Carlos first, then you."

"I've been your friend longer."

"He is, or will be, the father."

"Big deal," Jessica scoffed, "any male can be a sperm donor. I'm going to be the trendy godmother."

"Hey, that's my man you're calling *just* a sperm donor," Yasmin objected at the other end of the conversation.

"Whatever. I'm going to be the coolest auntie-godmother your kid could ever have."

Corked

"You are going to be a very bad influence on my sweet innocent child," Yasmin said. "I have to go to the pharmacy. Love you, *seesta*."

"Love you too. Call me as soon as you do the pregnancy test."

Chapter 32

Penticton

"In these trying times ...." the television droned in their hotel suite.

"Oh, please. Get a new phrase. Every single politician, businessperson, and ad writer has already overused that expression, and we are just at the start of this damn pandemic," Jessica groused.

After her FaceTime call with Yasmin, she had gone shopping, leaving Mike and Sparky at the hotel. Her excuse was she needed a new bra and she couldn't imagine him wanting to trail along behind while she poked through Walmart, one of the few stores allowed to remain open during the lockdown. Walmart sold groceries and prescription drugs, two things guaranteed to give them essential services status with the government boffins, while other smaller stores were closed for the duration. She could only imagine the financial mess that created for the independent retailers and the family-owned businesses.

Now, back at the hotel, she showered, applied a touch of makeup, paying special attention to her eyes, and dressed carefully in her new outfit. Checking her image in the mirror she winked at her reflection.

"Oh Mike," she sang out in a sultry, movie star voice.

"In here," he called from the living room.

"How do you like my new outfit?"

Mike turned his head to look and burst out laughing. She had one arm extended and resting against the door frame with her left leg coyly cocked.

"It's a very sexy look," he said taking in her outfit. "I particularly like the combination of a white dust mask, blue nitrile gloves, and black lacy lingerie," he said. "But, why do you have a jar of Nutella in your hand?"

"I believe in practicing safe sex," she replied, doing a sweeping Vanna White gesture with her hand starting at her shoulders and ending at her knees, "and Nutella is the hottest body-spread craze on Isla." Still channeling Vanna White, she removed her mask and brought the jar up to cheek level, displaying it with open palms and a cheesy pout on her lips.

"Say what?" Mike chortled.

Corked

"Yasmin told me that the Nutella spread has been locked up at Chedraui. Bored and amorous couples have been stealing it to experiment with this new craze." She opened the jar and dipped one finger in the spread, brought it to her lips and suggestively sucked on the finger. "Mmmm."

"Is this an offer of sex or lunch?"

"We could research this hot new trend while adhering to the safety guidelines," she said, running her tongue along her index finger.

Unbuttoning his shirt as he stood, Mike growled, "Come here, woman!"

Jessica giggled as he scooped her up in his arms and plunked her on the bed. He playfully nipped her fingertips, tugging off first one glove and then the other. He slipped one bra strap down and fluttered light kisses over her neck and breasts, then kissed her. "Mmmm, I like this research project." He said, gently kissing the tattoos on her left arm, a colorful collection of whale sharks, turtles and dolphins entwined with tropical flowers.

"Wait until we get to the Nutella part," Jessica murmured, just as her phone jingled with the tune assigned to Yasmin. "Oh damn, sorry, babe, I have to get this." She stretched sideways to grab the phone off of the nightstand.

Mike groaned and rolled away, "Really? It couldn't wait?"

She mutely shook her head and put the call on speaker, "Yassy, what's the news?"

"You're going to be an auntie."

"Oh my god, oh my god, I'm so excited." Jessica sat up and dropped her feet to the floor then perched on the edge of the bed. "Mike, Yasmin is pregnant."

Mike nodded, "I heard. Congratulations Yasmin, and Carlos too." He scrubbed his hand over his scalp and watched Jessica's face.

"*Gracias*, Mike," Yasmin answered.

"When is the baby due?" Jessica interjected.

"November, we think. I'll have a better idea once I see the doctor."

"So, you are only a month then?"

"*Si*, probably happened on my birthday. We had a nice romantic dinner and wine, too much wine," she said, happily.

"Have you picked out names yet?"

"No, not yet. We didn't expect to get pregnant so quickly."

"Carlos the Super Sperm!" Jessica exclaimed.

Mike sighed, and stood up. Jessica and Yasmin were settling in for a long phone conversation. He grabbed his underwear and pulled them on, then reached for his shirt and shrugged into it. As he zipped up his pants, he pointed at the kitchen to let Jessica know he was leaving the bedroom. Buttoning his shirt, he ambled to the refrigerator, pulled it open and lifted out a beer. "It's five o'clock somewhere," he muttered, twisting off the cap and flipping it into the garbage can.

Taking his beer to the sofa, he patted the cushions. "Come on Sparky, join me."

Sparky hopped up and rested his head on Mike's thigh, giving him the big old sad-eyed look that was usually a come-on for a belly rub, or a piece of steak.

"Sorry, bud, no steak, but I'll rub your belly," Mike took a pull on the bottle and swallowed. "At least one of us guys will have some fun."

The expression on Jessica's face while she talked baby stuff with Yasmin played over and over in his brain. Excitement. Happiness. A touch of envy. It was hard to pin it down. Whatever it was, they needed to have that talk. Do you want kids? He wasn't sure if Jessica felt the way he did, but he wanted to be with her permanently.

He had first approached her, several months ago, while she was watching the sunrise at Punta Sur with Sparky. When he got closer, he could see bruises on her face. She had recently been beaten, and badly. It wasn't until a few weeks later that he unearthed the pieces of the complicated story of

Jessica's abduction, confinement, and subsequent rescue. That morning at Punta Sur, he had spoken to her and seen the alarm in her face. Her fists were bunched and ready to defend herself while her eyes searched for an escape route. At that moment he had become fascinated by her spirit.

Realizing that he loomed over her, he had slowly squatted and aimed his attention at her dog. "He's a cutie. What's his name?"

"Sparky," Jessica had answered flatly, clearing hoping he would go away.

Extending the back of his hand for the dog to sniff, he'd shifted his attention to Sparky, "Hey, little buddy, do you want a scratch?" Sparky had seemed to understand what Mike was saying and had moved closer, letting him scratch his head, his rump, and then the sweet spot — the base of his tail.

Jessica had clearly not appreciated her dog befriending this stranger, but she had thawed just a little. "You know his name is Sparky, what's yours?"

"Miguel."

"Miguel?" She had considered his pale skin and green eyes, and replied, "You don't look, or sound, like a Miguel."

"You got me," he said. "My name is Mike Lyons."

227

Corked

"I'm Jessica," she'd said. Watching him scrutinize her injuries, she added, "You should have seen the other guy."

He had been smitten, and he had patiently waited as she grew to trust him. And now, he was terrified of scaring her away with a profession of his undying love. It was what he felt. Totally in love. Totally committed to her.

Pulling his thoughts back to the present he sighed and ruffled Sparky's ears. "What if she wants a family, Sparks? I'm going to be forty this year. Could I cope with kids?"

He couldn't verbalize his core fear. *What if she just didn't love him the way he loved her?*

Chapter 33

Penticton

"I'm not going to lie for you anymore," she shouted as she tossed her suitcase on the backseat and slammed the rear door so hard the SUV rocked back and forth.

"Please, darling, don't go," he begged. "I need you." He put his hand on the driver's door handle. "If you leave without me, the police will become suspicious."

She cursed and clouted his hand away, "Me, me, me. That's all you ever think about!"

His hand stung from the force of her blow, but he didn't complain. Instead, he tried again to convince her that he was acting in their best interests. "No, sweetheart, I wasn't thinking about me, I was thinking about our Marnie and her education. I'm frightened for her future."

"And why didn't you think of that before you gave that swindler all of our money?" She slapped at him again, and pushed past him into the driver's seat.

Corked

"Sweetheart, I explained my reason, Quartermain was offering an amazing rate of return on the investment." He reached to touch her arm in hopes of stopping her from leaving, but, fearful of her anger, he hesitated and let his hand drop.

"And you fell for it," she snarled. "You have put our family in a precarious financial situation, and you could end up in prison for life with no way to recoup our money."

He hung his head, and scuffed his shoe on the pavement, "I know. Please give me time. I'll figure it out."

"I lied for you!" She jabbed an accusing finger in his direction; spittle escaped her lips. "I told the police officer that my *darling* husband was with me all night. I told them you had drunk too much and eaten a large heavy meal and kept me awake all night with your sleep apnea and loud snoring," she searched for her keys. "What more do you want from me?" she yelled.

"Just wait a couple of more days and travel home with me," he pleaded as his eyes bounced toward the entrance door of the hotel. He fervently hoped no one could hear them. If word got out that they were heatedly arguing, it could become awkward.

Suddenly, she reached into the center console, grabbed three small plastic bottles and threw them in his face. "If you weren't so spaced on your drugs you could think more clearly."

He touched his face with his fingertips. "Please, sweetheart, I'll do anything you want, just don't go." He checked his fingers. *No blood.*

"Anything?" With one hand on the ignition button, she paused and studied his face. "Fine," she said, "as soon as we get back home, I'm filing for a divorce and you will not oppose it."

"All right, if that is what you really want." He had no intention of giving up so easily. He was certain he could calm her down and avoid a divorce. An expensive piece of jewelry usually did the trick, but this time their finances were a bit shaky and he would have to put it on a credit card, the one she didn't know about.

"Get out of my way, you fool!" She shoved the driver's door wide open and jerked her bag from the backseat.

"Of course, anything you want, dear," he said as he scurried ahead and held the lobby door open for her.

"I only want one thing," she said, her eyes pinned his. "You. Dead."

The fury in her face frightened him. He sucked in his breath; tears pricked at the corner of his eyes. *Surely not. She can't hate me that much.* "But I lov...."

She held up her hand. "Do. Not. Speak. Another. Word."

Anxiety made his pulse rapid and his breath short anxious puffs, but he remained silent as the elevator carried them to the third floor, then he rushed ahead to unlock their suite.

She stormed past him and headed straight to the bedroom with him pathetically trailing behind her. Just as his nose came even with the door frame, she violently swung the bedroom door shut. He hurriedly took a step back as he saw the slab of wood careening toward his face.

She hates me. My god, she really hates me.

Stunned by her rage, he shuffled to the armchair and crumpled onto it. Now, he had another problem. He had to figure out a way to save his business and the remaining family asset, their multi-million-dollar home in Windermere Estates, from the ravenous lawyers.

A chill swept through him: *A second time should be easier.*

If he did, it would have to be soon, before she talked to the lawyers, otherwise he would immediately move to the top of the suspect list. But then, it was common knowledge that in a suspicious death the police always suspected the spouse. *What should he do?*

Corked

His head pounded. He rested his elbows on his knees and massaged his throbbing temples.

Killing a person in the heat of the moment was one thing. But, to dispassionately plan the murder of his spouse, someone he had shared his life with for more than twenty years — that was a different proposition altogether. He rushed to the kitchen sink and threw up, then hastily rinsed his mouth out with water. With shaking hands, he flushed the disgusting mess down the drain.

Did he have the courage to kill her?

How would he do it?

He listened at the bedroom door. The television was on and he could hear her moving around in the bathroom. He quietly tiptoed across the hotel suite to his laptop. His hands hovered uncertainly over the keyboard.

He had heard bizarre stories about illegal services being available through something called the dark web, but that was beyond his comprehension. It was ludicrous for him — a respectable businessman, loving father, and supportive husband — to be searching for a hitman. But here he was trying to do just that.

How had his life become so complicated?

When they had met at the University of Calgary, his wife had been a stunningly beautiful and witty second-year student. He had been a

233

younger, gawky farm boy who was still getting accustomed to life in the city. She was planning to be a lawyer and he was studying business management, but after a brief and passionate romance their only child was created. Marnie was his treasured gift.

His wife had reluctantly given up her pursuit of a law career to stay home with the baby, but after a gap of several years she never returned to university life. Between working long hours at casual jobs to support his young family, he had continued his education and eventually graduated. Using the tiny nest egg of his parents' meager savings, he had started his own company.

His parents had given everything they had to get his business off the ground, and now twenty years later his angry and vengeful spouse wanted to take that away. It couldn't happen. His parents were both in an expensive care facility and he refused to downgrade their support just to satisfy her need to teach him a lesson.

He readily admitted that he had seriously blundered when he trusted Quartermain with their entire savings, and he had made a colossal and life-changing mistake when he had killed the man, but it had been an over-wrought emotional response to Quartermain's drunken taunting.

Now, he was cold-bloodedly considering having his wife murdered.

Corked

He heard the toilet flush and he hastily exited the web browser. He pulled up his Facebook page, pretending to cruise through the aimless drivel that was posted there, when the door to the bedroom jerked open. A nearby table lamp crashed to the floor the victim of a pillow, followed by a blanket lobbed from inside the bedroom.

"If you are going to stay in this suite, you can sleep on the couch tonight. I don't want you touching me, ever again!"

The bedroom door slammed shut a second time, like a cell door cutting off his freedom.

His feelings battered by his wife's anger and his need to protect himself by pretending everything was normal, he remembered he had a directors' meeting in one hour.

He scribbled a short note, explaining his absence, although he was quite certain she wouldn't notice.

Chapter 34

No Regrets Winery

Jessica hopped out of the sedan with Sparky hot on her heels.

Chris stood outside, leaning against the building absorbing the feeble warmth of the late afternoon sunshine.

She glanced at the parking lot. "Seems like a lot of vehicles. I thought the business had to remain closed until the lockdown is lifted," she said.

"The directors think the restrictions don't apply to them," Chris said. "They're here to pick up their free case allotments of the Chardonnay that we just bottled, and then tomorrow they head back to their own lives. Then they'll leave us alone for another six months."

"Do you know where Mike is? I don't want to traipse all over the property with Sparky in tow," she asked.

"Sorry, no idea. Try his cell phone."

Corked

She nodded and swiped the screen activating her phone. "Hey, Handsome. Sparky and I are outside the wine cellar. Do you have a minute?"

"Yep," he replied in her ear at the same moment that Sparky began to wiggle with excitement.

She looked in the direction that her dog's nose was pointed, and disconnected the call as Mike got within speaking distance.

"What's up?" he asked, leaning in for a smooch for her and a pat for Sparky.

She tilted her head to indicate that they should talk outside, and Mike nodded in understanding. Walking toward the vineyard she reached to grasp his hand, then remembered that was a restricted action under the new rules. *Well, frowned upon in public, but what they did in private was their own concern.*

"What are you grinning about?" he asked.

"Nothing," she winked at him. "I just wanted to talk to you about something I saw earlier today."

He waited.

"It's about Louise and Rodney Newcomb, the couple who are also staying at the Ramada," she clarified.

"Right, I remember. She's the one we've bumped into in the lobby a couple of times. She invited us for a drink in their room, then changed her mind because of the COVID-19 restrictions."

"Exactly."

"I haven't met him yet, have you?"

"No, I haven't. Anyway, Louise and a man, that I presume is her husband Rodney, were having a good old screaming match out behind the hotel," she said, "and at one point she tossed a handful of small items at him."

"Any idea what?"

"I couldn't see clearly, but it sounded like plastic, maybe plastic pill bottles."

"Odd," Mike said. "Why she would do that?"

Jessica rubbed her forehead then looked at Mike, "I think I remember her saying something about 'if you weren't so spaced on your drugs you could think more clearly' or something like that." She shook her head.

"We both know some couples like to argue and unless one or the other gets physical, there's not much anyone can do about it."

"I know," Jessica agreed, "except I think they were fighting about something to do with this place, and at one point I thought they were going to come to blows," she said. "I heard her scream at him about his poor investment decision, dumping their money into the winery. Louise also said, 'I'm not going to lie for you anymore,' then she got in the Jeep and slammed the door so hard it rocked on its springs. I left."

"Maybe he knew about the misappropriation of the money," he offered, "although, I can't think why he would cover up that unless ... he was in on the scam with Quartermain."

"That's my thought. He's guilty too."

Mike shook his head. "Nope, I don't think that's what happened. If she was yelling at him for losing their money, that means he likely didn't benefit from the theft." Thinking he looked down and dug the toe of his work boot into the dirt. "Too bad Sparky hasn't been able to solve this mystery," he joked.

"Who says he can't?" Jessica had an odd light in her eyes. "What if he just happened to give the board of directors a good old sniffy greeting when their meeting is done?"

"I'm not sure when their meeting is due to finish but if you are still here, we can give it a try," Mike agreed. "Why do you think it's one of them?"

"The biggest investors have the most to lose," she said.

"True, but some of those guys are too out of shape, or too old to wrestle with a guy the size of Quartermain."

Jessica gave Mike a sly look, "I told you before, even I could have done it."

"I remember," Mike agreed. He turned toward the hum of approaching voices. "Looks like you are in luck — that sounds like the meeting is over."

"Let's just casually stroll into the warehouse and you can introduce me," Jessica said as she started to walk toward the building.

She recognized the president and she waved and smiled as if they were good friends. He raised his hand in a half-hearted greeting, the expression on his face telling her he didn't remember her. That wasn't surprising; the only time they had met was when Quartermain's body had been discovered. Keeping Sparky by her side Jessica let Mike take the lead so that he could introduce her.

"Robert," Mike said, approaching a short blond man, "this is my friend Jessica Sanderson. She works in the vineyard. Jessica, this is Robert McLean."

"It's a pleasure to meet you, Robert," she said with a smile, glancing at Sparky to see if there was any reaction to Robert. Nothing. His eyes were aimed into the assortment of feet surrounding him.

"Nice to meet you too, and who is this?" he asked, looking down at her dog.

"Sparky," she said, tugging lightly on the lead to get his attention. "He's friendly; you can pat him."

"What type of dog is he?"

"Mexi-mutt."

He straightened and leveled his eyes on hers, "Mexi-mutt?"

"Yep, every type of dog that ever lived on the island where he was born is probably in his DNA, everything from Chihuahua to Great Dane."

McLean was about to respond when another of the directors interrupted him. The man reached out his hand, then pulled it back, "I'm sorry, shaking hands is a habit that is hard to break," he said. "I believe you have spoken to my wife, Louise, several times," he said, "I'm Rodney Newcomb. We're staying at the same hotel as you are."

"Yes, of course. So nice to finally meet you," she said. In her peripheral vision she noticed Sparky giving the man's shoes a thorough sniff. She waited to see what Newcomb would do or say.

"I'm sorry we had to cancel our invitation for drinks the other night. Something came up."

"Another time perhaps," she politely suggested.

"Um, yes, perhaps," Newcomb distractedly answered while watching Sparky. "Your dog seems to be fascinated by my shoes," he said.

Corked

Hearing the nervous edge in the man's voice, Jessica decided to increase his unease. "It's probably something that you walked in recently."

"What do you mean?"

"Sparky has a great nose for scents. You could have walked in something that he recognizes, like goose poop, or food, or maybe blood." She stuck a smile on her face that positively twinkled with peace, love, and good cheer to all men. *He's hiding something.*

Newcomb quickly lifted his right foot and examined the sole, then repeated the action with his left shoe. He appeared to be relived at what he saw, or perhaps, what he didn't see.

A smarter murderer would have dumped the shoes immediately, Jessica mused. Perhaps he was sentimental about his footwear, or maybe the shoes were expensive. Whatever the reason he seemed excessively concerned.

Mike tapped her elbow. "Jess, don't you have an appointment soon?" he asked.

She flicked a glance at him, and played along. "Yes, I do. Thank you for reminding me."

"I'll walk you out," Mike said.

"So nice to chat with you Rodney. I'm looking forward to getting to know you and Louise better," Jessica said.

"Yes, of course. Nice to meet you."

Mike put his arm around Jessica, pulling her closer and tipped his head to hers in a romantic pose as they strolled toward the Sonata. "Thoughts?"

"I think we're on to something. Sparky was very interested in his shoes, and dear Rodney near pooped his pants when I mentioned blood."

Stifling a guffaw, Mike agreed, "I saw that, so, now what?"

"I have an appointment to keep, remember? You just reminded me of it."

"I was only trying to get you away before the guy panicked and ran," Mike said, then added, "I'm curious. Sparky acted like he had never met the guy before, yet he is staying at the same hotel as us."

"He hasn't met him," she said, unlocking and opening the door for her dog to hop inside, "Sparky and I have run into Louise a bunch of times, but never Rodney."

"That makes sense."

"I'm going to phone Smith from the hotel."

"Oh, she'll be thrilled to hear from you," he rolled his eyes.

Jessica held up two fingers and intertwined them, "Corporal Smith and I are like that. Best buds. *Amigas.* Two peas in a pod."

Chapter 35

Penticton

"Smith here," a voice answered after the third ring.

"Corporal Smith, this is Jessica Sanderson," she said trying for a respectful tone in her voice.

After a pause, almost long enough for Jessica to think that Smith had disconnected the call, she answered, "Yes, Ms. Sanderson, what can I do for you?"

"I was wondering if we could meet for a few minutes? I think I have some information that might assist you with solving the murder of Kingsley Quartermain."

"If you have information germane to the investigation, we need you to come in and file a formal report," Smith said.

Jessica covered the phone with her palm and stifled a laugh. *Germane? Who uses that word in a conversation?* "Couldn't you just meet me please? I want to show you something that might be important."

"Where?"

"At the hotel where we're staying."

"Fine. Twenty minutes."

"Oh, and please bring that ballcap that was found at the winery."

"Why?"

"I'll show you when we meet up."

"Thirty minutes. I have to get the hat from the evidence locker."

"Okay great, see you in thirty," Jessica disconnected the call. "That went well," she said to Sparky, gesturing in a more-or-less motion. His tongue lolled out of the side of his mouth; he appeared to be smiling at her. "We've got some time, do you want to take a little walk along the river channel, bud?"

He jumped and laid his front paws on her knees, his tail wagging happily.

"Okay, let's go." She dressed Sparky in his warm jacket and clipped the lead to his collar. She sat on the couch and pulled on her boots then added her parka, hat, and gloves. "I'll be so glad when the weather warms up — I tired of having to wear all this gear every time you need a walk." She said to him.

"What was that all about?" Jones asked. He'd been listening to Caitlin's side of the conversation and had observed her annoyed expression.

Stuffing her cell phone in a pocket, and picking up the keys to her unmarked cruiser, Smith said, "Jessica Sanderson has requested a meet. She believes she has vital information that will solve our murder."

"Exciting," Jones stood and yanked on his heavy jacket. "I can't wait."

Smith wheeled the plain-Jane sedan into the hotel parking lot and put the transmission in park. She turned to Jones. "Do you remember the number of their suite?"

"402, but she's right there," he said as he pointed at the entrance, "with the dog."

"Yes, of course she is, Ms. Detective. Let's get this over with." Smith opened her door, and thumped her boots on the pavement then stood up and shut the door. She glanced at Jones to make sure he had shut the passenger's door, then hit lock with the key fob.

"Thank you for coming," Jessica greeted them.

"Our pleasure," Smith replied without smiling. Jones nodded.

"Please follow me; I have something to show you. Did you bring the baseball cap?"

"Yes, but it has to remain in the evidence bag."

Jessica kept walking until she was within sight of a large garbage container in the underground parking. She stopped and motioned for Sparky to sit. "I'd like to try an experiment with my dog," she said.

Smith arched her eyebrows and waited.

"I would like you to open the evidence bag and let Sparky have a good sniff of the cap."

"What exactly are you trying to prove?"

"Just bear with me, please."

Smith screwed up her lips, tilted a look at her partner, registered his nod, then took the evidence bag with the cap out of her pocket. She opened the bag and bent to allow the dog to smell inside.

"*Buscar*, Sparky," Jessica said, and unclipped his leash.

"What?"

"It's *search* in Spanish."

"He understands Spanish?" Smith remained bent over, and held the bag close to Sparky's nose.

"Yes, he was born on Isla." Concentrating on Sparky, Jessica didn't see the sideways look Smith gave her partner as she mouthed, *Spanish.*

"Now what?" Jones asked.

"*Buscar*, Sparky." Jessica repeated. He lowered his head so that his nose lightly skimmed the ground and he started a slow walk across the parking lot. Sniffing loudly and rapidly, he examined the area in great detail then he looped over to the garbage bin. He put his nose on a small object and inhaled deeply, breathing in the subtle nuances of the scent. His tail beat an excited rhythm.

"Good boy!" Jessica walked toward him and pointed to the discarded plastic pill bottles laying on the pavement. "I don't want to touch those, but they are exactly what I was hoping Sparky would locate with the scent from the ballcap."

Smith stood over the bottles. "Did you put these here?"

"No, but I know who did, and I think one or both of them are involved with the murder of Kingsley Quartermain."

"Who?"

"The name should be on the bottles. They're prescription drugs."

Jones pulled out his cell phone, and snapped several photos of the containers, their location in the parking lot, then using an evidence bag he scooped them up. Inside the bag, he turned them one at a time so that he could read the name of the patient and the medications. "They are all for a Rodney Newcomb. A heavy-duty anti-anxiety drug. A sleeping aid. And another heavy-duty anti-anxiety prescription."

"We need to go back to the detachment office and take a formal statement from you," Smith said to Jessica.

"We'll give you a ride," Jones said.

"All right, if that would be easier," she said, "but, may I bring Sparky?"

"Sure. He can sit in the back with you."

"Great. Give me five minutes to get my purse."

"We'll wait right here," Jones said, pointing to the entrance.

As Jessica and Sparky disappeared inside the lobby, Smith cut a look at Jones, and sighed.

"What?"

"We'll give you a ride," Smith simpered. "Oh, and bring your cute little doggie."

Jones chortled, subtly moved his right hand to waist height, and extended his middle digit, "Don't be a cranky cow. I just want to ensure that she comes to the detachment to make a statement."

"Right, and you can clean the muddy paw prints off the seats."

Jones laughed quietly. "You're just annoyed because she might be onto something — something that just might help solve our case."

Noticing Jessica walking toward the glass door, Smith cut off her intended response to Jones, the suggestion of a physically impossible action that he should do to himself.

Jessica pushed open the door, "Okay, all set."

Chapter 36

Penticton RCMP

Smith led the way into a brick building designed to look exactly like what it was, an RCMP police detachment. The stern exterior reminded Jessica of a fort, the type built in the eighteenth or nineteenth centuries as protection for the mounted police who patrolled the untamed wilds of Canada.

The federal police building sat squarely on the main street in the attractive tourist town in the heart of wine country. But there were no frivolous wine-themed exterior decorations that would have helped the austere façade blend with the tourism development plan. No empty oak barrels festooned with fake grapes, and no empty bottles, no hanging baskets brimming with flowers. Granted, it was March, but still, Jessica doubted that flowers were allowed to soften the forbidding building at any time of the year. There was no mistaking the message the dour exterior was intended to convey. It was a warning to all lawbreakers. We are one-hundred percent, abso-fricking-lutely serious.

"I'm sorry, what did you say?" Jessica asked, aware that Smith was staring at her.

Corked

"Coffee or tea," Smith repeated.

"A bottle of water, please."

Smith gestured to Jones to get the water, and he nodded and walked away. "Come with me," she said, leading the way to a door with a thick glass porthole-style window. "This room is available," she opened the door, and motioned Jessica inside.

Jessica involuntarily sucked in her breath and led Sparky inside the room. She clutched her purse, feeling the comforting outline of her cell phone. She had managed to text Mike with an update on where she was headed. It was silly to worry about being taken to a Canadian police station when she had done nothing more than annoy the lead detective, but repeated visits to the Mexican *policía* stations had made her wary. She stacked her hat, gloves and purse on the table, shucked off her winter jacket and hung it over the back of a chair, then sat down.

Jones opened the door and handed a bottle of water to her. "Thank you," she said, as she reached into her purse for Sparky's collapsible water dish.

"Stop!" Smith shouted, her hand demanding that Jessica freeze in place.

Jessica stopped, her hand still inside her purse.

"Remove your hand, slowly."

She complied, "I was only going to give Sparky some of this water," she explained. "I have a portable bowl for him in my purse."

Smith reached for the purse and turned it upside down, emptying the contents on the table. Her cell phone, a collapsible plastic dish, and a small zip-up wallet tumbled out. "You should have been searched before we came in here," Smith cut an irritated glance her silent partner.

"May I give Sparky some water?" Jessica asked.

"Yes," Smith pushed the articles toward Jessica.

Jessica opened the bottle, popped the plastic ring turning it into a bowl and poured a few ounces of water then set it on the floor beside Sparky. He lapped it up, then lay down beside her.

"Are you ready now?" Smith asked.

"Yes, what do you need?"

Smith turned on the recording device, stated the date and time, identified herself, as did Jones, and then she motioned for Jessica to do the same.

"Tell me in your own words why you suspect Rodney or Louise Newcomb are involved with the murder of Kingsley Quartermain."

Jessica huffed out a breath. "Well, it's a series of events actually. The morning that we found Mr. Quartermain my dog, Sparky, wandered off and was very interested in the ballcap that was on the floor behind a tank."

"I remember."

"Then recently I was at the winery with Sparky, and he was attracted to the shoes of Rodney Newcomb."

"He just *happened* to sniff the man's shoes?" Smith asked.

Jessica heard the skepticism in her voice, and she could feel the warmth of a blush creep up her throat. "I got him close enough to check the shoes of all the board of directors. He zeroed in on Newcomb."

"What made you think to get Sparky within sniffing distance?"

"It was just an idea that I had. I stopped by *No Regrets* and was talking to my partner, Mike. He's under contract with the company." She looked at Smith.

"Yes, we know," was the neutral reply.

"Okay, well, he mentioned the board of directors was meeting in the building," Jessica twitched her shoulders in an embarrassed shrug, "and I like to solve mysteries."

"Yes, we know that too," Smith confirmed.

Corked

"Oh." Jessica pinged her eyes from Smith to Jones and back to Smith, wondering how much they knew about her. Neither one reacted. She continued with her story. "When the embezzlement was discovered, I presumed that the people with the most money invested in the winery would be the ones with the strongest motive to kill Quartermain."

"Go on."

Jessica saw a flicker of annoyance on Smith's face. Was it because she was interfering in the investigation, or because she was taking too long to explain the circumstances? Either way, Smith was obviously not thrilled.

"I suggested to Mike that he introduce me to the directors, and I would let Sparky have a sniff around to see if he had any reaction. It was a spur of the moment decision."

Smith flicked a look at her partner and then scrutinized Jessica. "How did you make the leap in your deductions to include the prescription bottles."

"I overheard Rodney Newcomb and his wife Louise arguing about something to do with the winery, and at one point I thought the argument was going to get physical," she said. "Louise screamed at him about his poor investment decision, about dumping their money into the winery, then I heard a noise that turned out to be Louise tossing the plastic bottles at him."

Smith was silent.

Jessica continued, "I was hoping Sparky would confirm the scent on the baseball cap was the same as the scent on the pill containers. And I was pretty sure there would be a name printed on the labels." She studied Smith's expressionless face. *Cop-face*: the ability to blank your face so that the person they were questioning wouldn't know what the detectives were thinking.

Jessica continued, "Louise Newcomb also yelled 'I'm not going to lie for you anymore,' and I thought she might know something about the misappropriation of money, or she was covering for her husband in something much more serious." Jessica crossed her arms and leaned back in the hard chair, signaling she was done.

"Like murder."

"Yes, like murder," Jessica agreed.

"Thank you for your time. Constable Jones will give you and your dog a ride back to your hotel," Smith said, reaching to turn off the recording device.

Jessica held up her hand. "Just a moment; there is one other thing that might be related."

Smith stared at Jessica, and waited.

"When I was working on the bottling line at *No Regrets* with a local woman named Sharon

Hickey, she mentioned that she was almost t-boned by a vehicle on March 14th."

"And how does that relate to the murder?" Smith asked.

"She said she was coming home late that night and as she passed the lane leading to the winery a vehicle fishtailed into the intersection, almost hitting her."

"Did she get a license number?"

"I didn't ask."

"Make? Model? Color?" Smith probed.

"No idea of make and model, because I didn't ask," Jessica said, shaking her head, "but she did say it was a dark-colored SUV."

"Why do you think it is connected?"

"Someone driving erratically away from what we now know was a murder scene, late, on the same night that Quartermain was murdered?" Jessica made a bemused face. "It seemed suspicious to me."

Smith shot a look at her partner. He discreetly dipped his chin in a miniscule movement and blinked his eyes to signal that he agreed with Jessica. "Do you know how we can contact Sharon Hickey?"

"I imagine Ellen Taylor would have her phone number. Sharon said she gets called in to help out with the bottling from time to time."

"Right. Anything else you want to tell us?"

"Not that I can think of," Jessica said, "except, has my information been helpful?"

"I can't discuss an ongoing investigation, and I strongly request that you do not discuss these details with anyone else," Smith said, turned off the recording. She stood, nodded at Jones and left the room.

Jessica shook her head, picked up the empty water bowl, flattened it, and slipped it inside her purse. She tipped a look at Jones, "Brrr. I think another ice age just started."

His answering grin reassured her. "She's not that bad," he said, then added, "Come on, I'll give you and Sparky a ride back to your hotel."

Chapter 37

Penticton

"I should have bet you," Jones said as he sauntered back into the bullpen at the detachment, "that Jessica and her mutt would solve our case."

"The case is still unsolved, but now we have new information to follow," Smith retorted. "Let's bring Rodney Newcomb in for an official chat." She turned to Constable Natalie Garcha, "Nat, I'd like you to find Sharon Hickey and see if her information matches what Jessica told us about the SUV almost hitting hers. Check with Ellen Taylor at *No Regrets* for contact information."

"Will do," Natalie said, scanning her list of phone numbers then punching in the digits. "Good hunting," she said, as she placed the receiver against her ear.

"You've been watching American cop shows again, Nat," Jones joked.

Smith stood and pulled on her jacket. "You drive," she said.

"Yes ma'am," Jones saluted.

"Call me ma'am again and I'll get you reassigned to scrubbing out the drunk tank for a week."

"Yes, sir," he replied, grinning at her hollow threat. "How do you want to play this?"

"We'll give him the choice to voluntarily come with us, but if he refuses, we'll arrest him," Smith said.

"You think we have enough to hold him?"

"Not yet, but we'll have twenty-four hours to firm up the charges."

"No sleep tonight," Jones observed.

"Unless we can get him to confess, then yes, we'll work straight through the twenty-four hours."

"What about Louise Newcomb? She's his alibi, truthful or not."

"We pick him up first and start the questioning, then if we get something to work with, I'll send the uniforms to bring her in," Smith said.

As they walked toward their unmarked sedan, Jones thumbed a quick text to his wife, letting her know he was probably going to be working all night. Meaghan was familiar with their procedures and would understand the unstated reason, that the case was about to break open — or at least he hoped it would.

"All right then, let's go get our bad guy." He opened the driver's door and swung in behind the steering wheel.

Pulling into the hotel parking lot, Jones turned to Smith. "I was just here dropping off Jessica and Sparky," he said as pointed at the tower to the right of the main entrance.

"I know, but I didn't want us to drop off a witness, and then immediately pick up the suspect. It would have been difficult for Jessica."

"Ah, that's so sweet. You're being all kind and thoughtful," he simpered.

"Just being reasonable."

"Whatever you say, boss," he quipped. "Do you know which room he's in?"

"308," Smith opened the driver's door as soon as the vehicle had stopped. "I'm just going to check at the front desk that 308 is in the tower."

Jones got out, locked and stood beside the vehicle, his eyes scanning his surroundings. Penticton was a small and relatively safe city, and the inhabitants were helpful and friendly, but a cop always felt as if there was a target on their back. It was ingrained from the first day at boot camp. Never let your guard down.

He noticed a black, current year, Jeep Grand Cherokee with Alberta plates parked near the hotel tower. He unlocked his vehicle and typed the alphanumeric combination of the licence plate into his mobile computer.

Bingo! Rodney Newcomb, address Windermere Estates in Edmonton. Expensive vehicle and a seriously expensive home in a mega-million-dollar neighborhood. His business must be doing well, really well.

Jones started their vehicle and re-positioned it, hemming in the Jeep between the concrete wall and his sedan. *No sense making it easy for the guy if he decides to run.*

Two minutes later Smith appeared and raised a questioning eyebrow at his positioning of the sedan.

"That's his vehicle," Jones chinned toward the big black SUV.

"Good move. Let's go get him."

At Smith's request Jones took the lead on the interrogation of Rodney Newcomb. She hoped the guy-to-guy interaction would convince Newcomb to drop his guard, to open up to Jones.

"It's late. Why can't we do this tomorrow morning," Newcomb demanded.

"As we explained sir, this won't take long, we just have a few things to clear up." Jones replied.

Setting the requested bottle of water in front of the man, Jones identified himself, as did Smith, then he asked Newcomb, "Sir, could you please identify yourself for the purpose of this recording?"

"Do I need a lawyer?" Newcomb asked.

"Do you think you need a lawyer, Mister Newcomb?"

"Am I being charged with something?"

"Should we be charging you with something, sir?"

Smith watched the muscle in the man's jaw tick with frustration at the non-answers from Jones. He was within his rights to demand a lawyer, and then they would have to cease their interview. Surprising her, Newcomb suddenly barked out his name and then leaned back with a bored expression fixed on his soft features.

Good. He thinks he can outfox us. She clamped down on the smile that threatened to crack her stony expression. Her personal motto was taken from the Survivor game show: Outwit. Outplay. Outlast. Let's see how you do, *Mister Newcomb in an episode of Survivor, RCMP-style.*

Corked

"Thank you, Mister Newcomb. We asked you here today to help us clear up a few things," Jones said, beginning the lengthy process of establishing rapport with the man before gradually tearing apart his statement and alibi to dig out the truth.

Newcomb didn't reply.

"Could you please run through again where you were, and what you were doing on the night of March the 14th," he asked. "That would be the Saturday night after the shareholders' dinner at *No Regrets Winery*." Jones pretended to consult his notes, as if he had to refresh himself.

"As I have told you people before," Newcomb sighed impatiently, "my wife and I attended the barrel tasting of the red wines scheduled to be released in the fall. Then we had dinner together at Earls Restaurant, and I went to bed early. I wasn't feeling well."

Jones cocked his head, "Earls, love that place. What's your favorite dish there?"

"Thai curry chicken."

"Oh yeah, me too. With that great naan bread. Yum."

"Yes," Newcomb's eyes slid to the side, "it's very good."

Lie number one. Smith chalked up one mark on her mental score board.

"So, you had dinner, went back to the hotel, watched a little television, and went to bed," Jones said.

"No, I went back to the hotel and went directly to bed."

"Right, sorry about that. You see, I just can't go to sleep right after a big meal with alcohol."

"It wasn't a big meal. It was simply a bowl of rice and chicken with a few vegetables," Newcomb countered, "and I only had one glass of white with my dinner. I was driving and didn't want to exceed the .08 limit," he added.

Lie number two. Sanctimonious asshole.

"That's odd," Jones rustled through his files, then held up a page, "because, your wife, Louise, said you had been eating and drinking heavily and that you kept her awake all night with your loud snoring and sleep apnea." He pointed at the paper and gave Newcomb a perplexed look.

"She's mistaken. I ate and drank a lot at the shareholders' dinner the night before."

"Right, I can see how she would get confused," Jones agreed sympathetically.

"Constable Jones," Smith said.

"Yes ma'am?"

Smith knew he was messing with her again, with the 'yes ma'am'. "I would like to speak to you

265

privately please," she said, tipping her head toward the door.

"Yes ma'am, certainly ma'am. For the record, this interview is being suspended. Constable Jones and Corporal Smith are leaving the room," he intoned, reciting the time and shutting off the equipment.

They locked the door behind them and moved into the soundproof observation room. Smith thumped him on the bicep and muttered, "Stop the ma'am crap!"

Jones stifled a grin. "He's lying already," he said.

"Yes, I think we can break him quickly. I want to bring his wife in right now."

"I agree. Who's going? You or Natalie?" Jones asked.

"I'll send Natalie and a uniform to pick her up, and put her in an adjoining room. We'll have to arrange for one of us to leave the room just long enough for the door to be open while Natalie and Louise Newcomb walk past. I want Newcomb to see her being brought in for questioning," Smith said.

Jones caught the look in his partner's eyes; they were shining with anticipation.

The huntress was on the prowl.

Chapter 38

Penticton

Dressed in a robe and slippers, Louise Newcomb shuffled into the tiny galley kitchen. She poured a serious dollop of whiskey, neat, into a glass and shakily sat down at the table. The two RCMP detectives had arrived at their suite and requested Rodney come to their office, for a formal statement. When they knocked, she had instinctively checked the time on the bedroom clock, nine-thirty. It couldn't be a good thing if the police felt they had to speak to Rodney late at night.

She tipped back the drink and inhaled a mouthful.

She had lied to the police when she provided Rodney with an alibi. In truth, she was fast asleep when he blundered into the suite, weeping a confession about striking Quartermain in a moment of white-hot rage and letting him die. Until that moment she never thought he would, or could, be capable of killing anyone.

Corked

March 14th had been a physically draining day. Quartermain had hosted a barrel sampling of the upcoming vintages, accompanied by numerous tapas-style dishes, and stilted conversation between the investors who were for the most part strangers to each other. She had played her part as a minor celebrity, the spouse of one of the directors. She greeted everyone pleasantly, inquired politely about their lives, and smiled until her face hurt and she'd hated every minute of it.

She had left as soon as possible, with Rodney staying behind for the final meeting with the directors and Quartermain. They were planning to fire him for the misappropriation of funds. What had actually happened at that meeting, she had no idea; all she knew is the night ended with her soon-to-be-ex-husband killing Quartermain.

Louise pulled their shared laptop toward her. She needed something to take her mind off of what was happening at the police station. A little Spider solitaire might help to settle her nerves.

Opening the laptop, she noticed the browser already had two tabs open, one for Facebook and one for another unfamiliar page. She was about to close the second tab but something niggled at her. She clicked on it, then hovered the cursor over history.

Her breath caught in her throat. No! He wouldn't, would he?

Constable Garcha led Louise Newcomb into the dour brick building. "Just follow me please, ma'am. This won't take long," she said. Louise reluctantly followed the younger woman.

"Louise?" She turned her head sharply toward the plaintive sound of Rodney's voice and caught a fleeting glimpse of his anxious face as the door to another room closed.

"In here, please, Mrs. Newcomb," Garcha said, indicating a plain room furnished with only a metal table and three plain chairs. "Would you like a cup of coffee or tea?"

Louise shook her head. "No thank you. I want a lawyer."

"You aren't being charged with anything Mrs. Newcomb. We would just like to clear up a few details," Garcha said, repeating a well-worn phrase, meant to calm the detainee's fears.

"I know my rights," Louise stated, dredging up remnants of her long-ago beginning law education. "I want a lawyer."

Garcha felt a prickle of disappointment. She had been looking forward to interrogating the woman. Now she would have to wait for the lawyer to appear and at this time of night it could take a while. "Yes ma'am, I'll bring you a phone." Shutting the door on Interview Room #2, she sent a message to Smith, advising her of Louise Newcomb's demands.

Smith texted back: "Okay."

An hour later Daryl McDougall presented himself at the RCMP station. "I'm representing Louise Newcomb," he said.

Garcha recognized him as one of the junior partners in a local firm. She escorted him to the interview room where Louise was waiting and left them to their discussions. She sighed deeply, unwound her bun, dug her fingers into her scalp, to restart her brain as Jones had joked, and twisted her hair back into a knot that settled at the base of her neck. Feeling the heavy weight on her neck, she was tempted once again to make an appointment to have her hair cut into an easier style. Garcha rotated her shoulders and neck through a few stretching exercises. She bent over, relaxing into the stretch and then straightened up.

She was tired, but they were headed into an all-nighter with Rodney and Louise Newcomb unless the lawyer walked them both out. She sat at a desk, extended her legs, and leaned back with her hands behind her head.

Corked

A sharp rap on the inside of the metal door startled Garcha out of her micro-nap. She stood and opened the door to Interview Room #2.

"Yes, Mr. McDougall?"

"My client would like to speak to your supervisor."

"Yes, sir." Garcha popped a text to Smith; "Newcomb and lawyer want to talk to you."

A smiley face appeared in seconds, then the door opened and Smith gave Garcha a thumbs up. She whispered, "What's happening?"

"No clue," Garcha quietly admitted. "Daryl McDougall arrived thirty minutes ago and conferred with Louise Newcomb then he told me that his client wanted to speak to my supervisor."

"Let's hope this is the breakthrough we need, and not McDougall taking his client out of here," Smith settled her features into an unreadable mask and entered the room, followed by Garcha.

"Good evening, I'm Corporal Smith, General Investigative Section, GIS, of the Penticton RCMP," she said. "I was told you wanted to speak to me." Smith said, "and for the purposes of protecting everyone in this room, we are going to record the conversations so please identify yourselves."

"Louise Newcomb."

"Constable Natalie Garcha."

"Daryl McDougall, I'm representing Mrs. Newcomb."

"I don't understand, Mr. McDougall. We haven't charged Mrs. Newcomb with anything; we merely asked her in to help us clear up a few details."

McDougall gave Smith a knowing look. He wasn't fooled by her statement. "Regardless, she felt that she needed legal representation."

"What did you want to speak to me about, Mrs. Newcomb?" Smith asked. She wasn't going to waste time sparring with the legal-beagle.

Louise Newcomb shot a look at McDougall and he nodded. "I was mistaken about my husband's alibi," she said, not admitting that she had outright lied. "I was asleep all evening and don't know when he returned to the hotel." She knew exactly what time her weeping husband had awakened her, but her instinct was to protect herself.

"Are withdrawing your alibi for your husband, Mrs. Newcomb?"

"Yes," she said.

Smith decided to reveal a bit of information they had held back to see Louise Newcomb's reaction, "Mrs. Newcomb, are you aware of how Mister Quartermain died?"

"I heard on the news that he was hit over the head with something heavy, maybe a bottle?"

"Yes, that's what we released to the press; however, there was more."

Louise jerked in her chair and asked, "What more?"

"The blows to his head didn't kill him. He was dragged into the wine cellar, tied to the tines of the forklift, hoisted high enough that his feet couldn't touch the floor, and he strangled to death." Smith stonily appraised the woman's pale face, watching as shock and disbelief played over her features. "It was deliberate," Smith confirmed.

"No, that's not what he tol ...," Louise stammered out, then stopped.

"Not what he told you, Mrs. Newcomb?" Smith asked.

"I ..."

"Don't say anything more, Louise," the lawyer cautioned. "I want immunity for my client if she cooperates with you."

Smith said, "I'll have to wake up someone who can make that deal."

"We'll wait," McDougall said, causing Smith to almost smile at the comment.

Yes, they would wait. Until she was ready to charge Louise Newcomb as an accessory after the fact, or the twenty-four hours had lapsed.

Corked

Smith shut off the recording, and departed with Garcha. "Fill Jones in on what's happening. I have to wake up our boss, and the prosecutor," Smith said as she listened to the superintendent's cell phone ringing.

Chapter 39

Penticton

Ninety minutes later, Smith re-entered the room with Garcha and turned on the recording machine. She stating the time and date, noting they were now in the early hours of March 24th.

"Mrs. Newcomb," Smith said, "we have approval from the prosecutor. If your information is sufficient to help us close this case, you are exempt from prosecution for the murder of Kingsley Quartermain."

Louise sighed and dropped her head; tears tracked down her face and her chin wobbled. "Rodney wanted to have me killed," she whispered.

"I'm sorry. Please repeat that." Smith was shocked. This wasn't at all what she had been expecting. "Please speak louder for the recording."

Louise pulled her head up and made eye contact with Smith. "He wanted to have me killed," she repeated, clearly this time.

"How do you know?"

"Our laptop. The history showed him searching for murder for hire and hitmen," she bawled out the words, "A hitman! For me, his wife, the mother of his only daughter."

"Why do you think he was planning to have you murdered?"

Louise turned her head sideways, "I told him I wanted a divorce."

"Why do you think your husband wanted to have you killed instead of just getting a divorce?" Smith was sure there a stronger reason than a simple divorce. She was convinced Louise Newcomb was still holding back, trying to portray herself as a good person.

Louise sobbed, "I said I wouldn't lie for him anymore. He admitted to hitting Quartermain, because we'd lost all of Marnie's university tuition," she gasped out. "Now you tell me that he deliberately killed Quartermain, that it wasn't an accident. I don't know him anymore. He's not the man I married. He's a monster," she exclaimed.

"Mrs. Newcomb, is your laptop joint property?" Smith asked.

"Yes, why?"

"May we have your permission to retrieve it from the hotel and search for the information that you just provided us?" Smith asked, then explained, "Permission from you is quicker than waking up a judge and obtaining a search warrant."

"Yes."

"Where in the hotel suite would we find the laptop? And what brand is it? I want to be sure we take the correct laptop."

"There is only one, it's an HP and it is sitting on the table," she muttered. "May I have a few tissues, please?"

"Yes, of course," Smith motioned to Garcha who slipped out to retrieve a box. "Is the laptop password protected?" Smith continued.

"Yes, it's our daughter's name, Marnie."

After being a police officer for several years, Smith was unsurprised. Many people were careless with their private information and using a child's name as a password was as inadequate as no password at all. Instead of lecturing the woman she neutrally responded, "Thank you."

Repeating the procedure of verbally signing out of the interview, Smith left the room, and dispatched a constable to retrieve the laptop from the hotel.

Jones was head down on his desk, snoring softly. Smith tapped him on the shoulder. "Yep," he answered, wearily sitting up and stretching his arms overhead. He yawned hard, and she heard his jaw creak in protest.

"We're getting the laptop from the hotel. Mrs. Newcomb says Rodney was searching for a contract killer on the web. She believes he wants her dead."

"Holy hell, that came out of left field," Jones was now wide awake. "Why?"

"According to Louise Newcomb, her husband apparently attacked Quartermain over the loss of their daughter's university tuition. She told Rodney she wasn't going continue to lie and be his alibi, and a she wanted a divorce. I think he was overwhelmed by events, and looking for what he saw as a solution," Smith replied.

"That's great," Jones said, and cracked another wide yawn that sounded as if he was trying to dislocate his lower jaw.

"I helped Louise Newcomb along a bit, by explaining that Quartermain was alive when he was hung from the forklift," Smith had a tiny smile that ticked one side of her mouth up. "She didn't know that he had lied to her about that, and now she's quite willing to cooperate."

"Great work, partner," Jones said, giving her a tired lopsided smile. "At this rate, we might be able to crash into bed before noon."

"Maybe," Smith agreed, as she slumped into a chair beside Jones. "Oh, man, I need a hit of caffeine, but I literally can't stomach any more of this awful stuff we call coffee. I would pay anything for a cup of Starbucks right now."

"Amen to that."

"Is this what you are waiting for?" A young constable asked, holding out a laptop for Smith.

"Looks like it," she agreed, taking the computer. "Thanks. Time to continue our chat with Mrs. Newcomb."

Jones scrubbed his face, asking, "What do you want me to do?"

"Check on Rodney Newcomb. I'll join you as soon as I can confirm Louise Newcomb's assertion that her husband was looking to hire a killer."

Jones opened the door to Interview Room #1 where Rodney Newcomb was losing the battle to stay awake. His head jerked twice as he drifted in and out of an uncomfortable inertia.

"Mr. Newcomb," he said purposely louder than necessary, causing the man to snap upright.

"What?"

"We are going to continue with your statement. Do you need a bottle of water? Or coffee?"

"No, I need to take a leak."

"Of course, come with me." Jones had expected this request; after all the man had been inside the room for going on seven hours, but this is where things could get tricky. Newcomb wasn't under arrest and once he was up and moving around, he could decide to leave the station. If he did, they would then detain him on suspicion of murder, and quite certainly Newcomb would demand to have a lawyer present — resulting in another delay.

Jones knew Smith was confident she had the key to unlock Newcomb's confession. She had the laptop and the search history, plus his wife had rescinded her alibi for him. Still, he wanted the man to voluntarily stay until they were certain of their evidence. Jones escorted Newcomb to the washroom and hung around outside the door as a precaution in case he decided to bolt.

While Rodney Newcomb was in the men's room, Smith opened the door to Interview Room #1 and shot a questioning glance at Jones.

"Bathroom break," he said.

She patted the laptop, saying, "Let's resume as soon as he's finished." Smith entered the room where Rodney Newcomb would shortly, in her opinion, be confessing to murder. She tucked the laptop out of view.

Newcomb re-entered, stopped and gave Smith a bleary-eyed glare, "I'm tired. I want to go to bed."

"I understand, sir. Please bear with me, I just have a couple more questions to ask you and then we're done."

He sank to the chair saying, "Make it quick. I'm exhausted."

Smith quickly went through the procedures to resume the interview, then pulled out the computer. "Do you recognize this laptop, Mr. Newcomb?"

"What?" he stammered out. "No! Should I?"

"You don't sound too certain, sir. Let me show you the sign-in screen," Smith turned the device so that he could see the photo of his daughter. "I believe your password is Marnie, your daughter's name. Would you type that in for me, sir?"

"No."

"Very well," Smith typed the letters and the browser opened. "This is your laptop isn't it, Mr. Newcomb?"

"You don't have my permission to touch my computer! You need a warrant," he excitedly declared.

"Your wife, Louise Newcomb, gave us permission and the password, Mr. Newcomb."

Sobbing, Newcomb placed his elbows on the table and his face in his palms, "Louise, why? Why?"

Smith waited until his sobbing quieted. "Your wife is unhappy that you were searching for someone to kill her. She has also rescinded her alibi for you. She stated that she has no idea what time you returned to your hotel suite on the night of March 14th."

"I want a lawyer," Newcomb said, pulling himself a little straighter.

"Are you certain Mr. Newcomb, wouldn't it be better for you to get this off your chest, to tell the truth?" Smith asked. A confession was the cleaner, preferred resolution to a murder investigation, but it was rarely the outcome of their hard work.

"Lawyer."

She'd take what she could get.

"Rodney Newcomb, I am arresting you for the murder of Kingsley Quartermain," Smith intoned. "You have the right to retain and instruct counsel without delay. You also have the right to free and immediate legal advice from duty counsel," she added, "Do you understand?"

Newcomb remained silent.

"Sir, do you understand?" Smith repeated.

"Yes."

"Do you wish to call a lawyer?"

"Yes."

Chapter 40

Penticton RCMP

Smith motioned for Jessica to join her outside on the concrete bench, and handed her a cup of coffee from the staffroom. "It's not Starbucks. They're closed until further notice, because of the lockdown," she said. "Be warned, this stuff tastes like something you'd find in a toilet," her lips tilted in a half-smile.

"Thank you, Corporal Smith," Jessica replied, motioning for Sparky to lie at her feet. She sat on one end of his leash, and took the hot cup from Smith with both hands. She didn't know why she had been summoned to the RCMP detachment on Main Street, but sitting outside sharing a convivial coffee with the senior detective was not the first reason that came to mind.

"Caitlin." Smith stretched her legs out, and tilted her face to the weak spring sunshine.

"Okay, Caitlin." Jessica cautiously sipped the hot liquid and stifled the urge to spit it out. "Thank you for the coffee, but it tastes awful," she said, balancing the still-full cup on the bench between them.

"Yeah, drinking this is a mandatory part of the twenty-six-week RCMP training," Caitlin said, without moving her head or opening her eyes. "When we get sent to bootcamp in Regina we have to sleep with the windows open in all types of weather, run and train until we puke, and drink this shit to prove we're tough," she took another slurp of the dark liquid.

"If you can drink this stuff, you've got my vote. You're tough," Jessica replied, and poured hers onto the ground.

"You're right," Caitlin agreed, straightened up, then dumped hers out as well. "It's disgusting."

"Yep," Jessica consciously breathed slower, releasing the tension she had been holding in her chest. Maybe this woman wasn't such a humorless grump after all.

"You probably heard on the news, we charged Rodney Newcomb with the murder of Kingsley Quartermain."

"Yes, I did, congratulations."

"Thank you for your information; it was helpful," Caitlin said.

Surprised by the warmth in Caitlin's voice Jessica gushed, "Thank you, that's so nice of you."

Caitlin ignored the comment and continued, "But I have to say, you're an annoying and interfering busybody."

"Yes, so, I've been told," Jessica acknowledged, "by several Mexican policía."

"And yet you keep meddling in murder investigations," Caitlin said, a smile softening her criticism. "Now, tell me how you knew about the treasure that you and your friend found on Isla Mujeres."

"Oh, that," Jessica replied, with an airy shrug of one shoulder. "We had a night of too much tequila and Yasmin told me some of her grandmother's stories. According to Maria Guadalupe Medina the family is related to *La Trigueña*."

"La what?"

"*La Trigueña*, the brunette. A young island woman whom the middle-aged pirate Fermin Mundaca was head-over-heels in love with, but she wasn't attracted to him. She married a much younger man instead."

Caitlin turned her full attention to Jessica. "How did that connect to the treasure?"

"Long story, but basically Isla Mujeres was a favorite hideout for marauding pirates, and one particularly successful pirate, Captain Boudewijn de Graaf buried some of his treasure on the island in the 1680s. It was found by Mundaca and moved to his estate. Yasmin and I rediscovered it." She made a dismissive face, as if it was an everyday occurrence to uncover pirate loot. "Honestly though without Sparky's help we probably wouldn't have found the treasure." Sparky lifted his head when he heard his name and Jessica ruffled his ears. "Such a smart little man, aren't you sweetie?"

"He actually found the treasure?"

"Yes, he dug up several coins, a few loose jewels, and a beautiful jewel-encrusted crucifix."

"That's a fantastic story."

"Except we didn't get to keep anything."

"So, I heard," Caitlin said.

"The most beautiful piece was the crucifix," she said, remembering the feel of the stunning artifact nestled in the palm of her hand. "It was studded with jewels set into what appeared to be solid gold."

"What happened to it?"

Jessica slid Caitlin a side-eyed look, "I'm not sure I should admit anything to a police officer," she deadpanned.

Surprised, Caitlin gave Jessica a penetrating look.

Jessica's eyes crinkled and her mouth twitched. "It's not what you think. We didn't keep it. Yasmin and I left it for the padre in the collection box, and he's still trying to figure out how it got there."

"That is funny, but didn't the authorities ask about it?" Caitlin asked.

"No, they didn't know exactly what we had found. We decided the crucifix belonged in a church."

"I'll deny ever saying this, but I think that was a good decision."

"I think so too," Jessica nodded.

"And your propensity to get in the way of police investigations, how did that come about?" Caitlin asked.

Jessica gave her a look, the one that she knew made Mike laugh, and put her hand flat on her chest. "Me?" she asked innocently.

As predicted, Caitlin chuckled. "Yes, you. Don't play all innocent with me."

"I'm going to put the blame on Sparky. His nose is typically the reason we get involved in … um … events," she said.

Caitlin shook her head and made eye contact with Sparky, "Your momma is a big fat liar, pooch. She thinks she's smarter than us poor overworked police officers."

"Not true. He's the smart one of this duo."

"Changing the subject, how long are you and Mike staying in Penticton?" Caitlin asked.

Jessica turned thoughtful. "It all depends on his job. The board of directors at *No Regrets Winery* are scrambling to sort things out financially, and I'm not sure they can afford to keep Mike on," Jessica said. She decided to remain quiet about the deliberate mislabeling incident. New friend or not, Caitlin was a police officer, and Jessica didn't want to add more problems to the current situation.

"Doesn't he have a contract?"

"Yes, but with everything that's happening in the world, it isn't worth the paper it's written on," Jessica replied, using one of her dad's favorite expressions.

"It would be valuable if it was written on toilet paper," Caitlin quipped as she cut an amused glance at Jessica and the two of them burst into laughter.

"It'd be priceless," Jessica agreed.

Caitlin pulled her RCMP business card out of a pocket and scribbled a series of digits on the back, then handed it to Jessica. "This is your Get Out of Jail Free card," she said, referring to the once popular board game of Monopoly. "That's my private phone," she said poking a finger at the numbers.

"Thank you, Caitlin, that's very generous of you."

Caitlin tipped her head, and gave Jessica a look, a mix of are-you-really-that-gullible and of-course-I'm-fabulous. "You understand I can't actually spring you from jail, right?"

Jessica pondered a moment. "Yes, I get that. However, being able to brag to my friends that I have an RCMP Corporal on speed dial, that's gotta be worth something."

Caitlin shook her head, "I said you were annoying, but I meant that you are a huge pain in the ass."

"Absolutely. Wanna do lunch sometime?"

"Sure, once the lockdown is lifted."

"We have a little kitchen at our hotel suite. Mike and I could create something edible, well, Mike could create something edible. I specialize at setting the table, serving drinks and providing scintillating conversation."

Caitlin held her hand out. "Give me back my card."

Jessica clutched the card, holding it away from Caitlin. "Already? I haven't done anything, yet."

"I'll add my personal email address," she said.

Chapter 41

No Regrets Winery

Ellen sighed and shot Mike a searching look. He offered her an encouraging smile. "I don't know," he said in response to her earlier question about what did he think the directors were going to decide.

She felt like a naughty school girl waiting outside the principal's office, only in her case she was waiting for a quintet of wealthy middle-aged men to decide her future — more than just her future. This was decision day for everyone who worked at, or had invested in, the winery. Would they continue to throw cash into the struggling business, or would they decide to sell off the assets to recoup some of their money?

She drew in a deep breath, exhaled and turned to face Mike, "Mike, I just wanted to say I'm so sorry."

"You're sorry, why?"

She flapped her hand uncertainly, "For getting you involved in our mess."

"What do you mean, Ellen?"

"This. The financial mess. The wine swap. It can't be good for your reputation," she said.

Mike smiled, his face lit with humor and understanding, "I've seen worse, Ellen, 'way worse, and while I don't condone selling a wine as a different varietal of grapes, it's in the past, and I'm not going to blow the whistle," he said, unconsciously mimicking the phrase that Ellen had used when she told the accountant about the share scam. "As you know, Ben quit, and Chris stayed on but he feels badly about the deception, and going forward I think he will be a loyal and hard-working employee."

Ellen looked down, fiddled with her phone, then reluctantly met his eyes again. "But what will you do if the directors cancel your contract and shut us down?"

"I'm not worried, Jessica and I are both very adaptable and resilient," Mike said. "We'll figure something out."

The End

The backstory of Isla's Elmo

"Cool. We're invited to a Halloween party October 31st 2011, at Villa la Bella," my husband Lawrie Lock said as he read the invite. A month later the local postman arrived at our door on his delivery moto with an enormous cotton sack tagged with Lawrie's name and address.

"What the heck is that?" I was oblivious to Lawrie's recent online shopping.

"That" was an Elmo costume shipped from the manufacturer in Lima Peru; a crimson red furry costume, complete with big head and googly eyes.

Years ago, when Lawrie's eldest grandson was learning to talk, he called him Elmo, and the nickname stuck. The boys were coming for a visit in December 2011 and Lawrie decided he could get double duty from the costume; the Halloween party and greeting our grandsons at the passenger ferry.

The Elmo costume was a huge hit. In the next two years it was used many times over by Lawrie when he greeted family and friends at the ferry docks. Elmo-

Corked

Lawrie was also invited to the first anniversary party of Barlito's restaurant on Hidalgo Avenue. Everyone wanted their photos taken with Elmo, even a few of the dubious characters that hang around the streets late in the evenings.

In 2013 our friend Freddy Medina asked if he could borrow the costume for a special young boy's birthday fiesta. Freddy was so overwhelmed by the happiness of the young lad that he suggested a Christmas parade featuring Elmo and our newest character costumes, Mickey and Minnie Mouse, purchased for another Halloween party at Villa la Bella.

The first parade in 2013 was hilarious. There were only about eight or nine vehicles and a dozen or so motos neatly lined up facing north. Our jefe, Freddy was late. When he arrived, he instructed us to turn around, we would be heading south into the densely populated neighborhoods.

What did we know? We were all new at this parade stuff.

The parade bounced through the colonias on a higgledy-piggledy route that the driver of the lead vehicle had mapped out in his head. We had absolutely no idea what we were getting into. As we noisily passed, adults ran to find the kids to come see Elmo, Mickey, Minnie, Sponge Bob, clowns and the Grinch.

2013 was also the year that we learned not to get out of the golf carts in our costumes. Lawrie had waded into the crowd to say "hi" to the kids, when a group of inebriated men thought it would be uproariously funny to lob Mickey Mouse in to the air and catch him – a few times. Picture this: a large man in a mouse costume tossed up and down in a crowd! Only in Mexico!

Two hours later our tired group disbanded in centro on Rueda Medina. Elmo's vehicle happened to park near the assembly point for the Municipal Presidente of Isla's Christmas Cavalcade. The Presidente *suggested* to Freddy Medina that Elmo should join that parade. Freddy who had just spent two hours dancing in the back of a pickup truck wearing the fur suit was soaked through to his underwear with perspiration. However, one does not say no to the Presidente. And away he went, dancing and shouting Feliz Navidad for another two hours.

In 2014 we had more people join the parade bringing the total to about twenty vehicles. Freddy arranged for the funny bus for participants who didn't want to drive but wanted to be part of the event. The funny bus was a two-level dilapidated vehicle, decorated with colored lights and blasting loud music. It haunted the island streets for a few years, the operator charging a small amount to take people on after-dark tours.

That year we followed a route dictated by the height of the double-decker. The low hanging electrical wires are always a challenge in Mexico. The normal solution is to have a person stand on the top of a truck or vehicle with a wooden broom to lift the wires out of the way. Yep, lift live wires with a broom! But in a parade there just isn't time to lift every low hanging line and sneak past, while the upper deck passengers duck below the seatbacks. It was easier to find a different route.

2015 was the first year that we had a motorcycle police escort who tried their best to keep us all together. Some of the vehicles broke down. A few drivers turned the wrong way. And still others had non-parade vehicles cut in between, causing more confusion. The excited youngsters and their smiling parents made it all worthwhile.

And then there was the 2016 parade, Saturday December 17th, our 4th Annual Christmas Caravan. We had a collection of about fifty trucks, cars, motorcycles, and golf carts. We had Elmo, Santa, Mrs. Claus, Mickey, Minnie, a Ninja Turtle, and several dogs including Sparky. There were dozens of Santa hats, decorations

Corked

bought, and decorations handmade. Music. Lights. Candy.

Without the now-defunct funny bus, our route was more flexible. We wound south through the neighborhoods of Salina Chica, Salina Grande, Las Glorias, and through narrow side streets along the main road. Then we turned into the colonias across from the marinas, popped out onto the main road by Chedraui store and headed back toward centro. Next our leader took us on a crosshatch route through all of the streets in centro to wave at tourists and locals. Our faces hurt from smiling. Our throats were dry from laughing. It was the best parade yet.

In December 2017 Lawrie and I made a quick trip back to Canada. He was having health issues and we sensed that this might be his last chance to celebrate a family Christmas. Rob and Julie Goth happily stepped in to become the new Mickey and Minnie for the parades.

A few months after Lawrie's death, Freddy and his wife Yadira (Eva) Velázquez arrived at my home. "I want to rename the parade in honor of my good friend Lawrie," he said. I was speechless.

Freddy continued, "Without his help this parade would never have happened and I want everyone to remember him."

I explained how Lawrie's grandsons called him Elmo and we decided on Elmo's Christmas Caravan - La Caravana Navideña de Elmo because it translated well into Spanish.

As for the Elmo costume of the 2011 Halloween party, has a permanent home with Freddy. Thank you, Freddy Medina for being the good-hearted, crazy person who thought up this event and for honoring my sweetie with changing the name to Elmo's Christmas Caravan.

The original Isla Mujeres Elmo-Lawrie Lock still rides with us in spirit.

About the author

Born in a British Columbia Canada gold mining community that is now essentially a ghost town, Lynda has had a diverse, some might say eccentric, working career. Her job history includes bank clerk, antique store owner, ambulance attendant, volunteer firefighter, supervisor of the SkyTrain transit control center, partner in a bed & breakfast, partner in a microbrewery, and hotel manager. The adventure and the experience were always more important than the paycheck.

Writing has always been in the background of her life, starting with travel articles for a local newspaper, an unpublished novel written before her fortieth birthday, and articles for a Canadian safety magazine.

When she and her husband, Lawrie Lock, retired to Isla Mujeres, Mexico in 2008, they started a weekly blog, Notes from Paradise, to keep friends and family up to date on their newest adventure.

Needing something more to keep her active mind occupied, Lynda and island friend Diego Medina self-published two bilingual books for children, The Adventures of Thomas the Cat / Las Aventuras de Tómas el Gato plus The Adventures of Thomas and Sparky / Las Aventuras de Tómas y Sparky.

Well, one thing led to another and Lynda created and self-published the Isla Mujeres Mystery series, set on the island in the Caribbean Sea where they lived. Following the death of Lawrie in 2018, she and Sparky remained in Mexico until the COVID-19 pandemic became a reality.

In March of 2020 Lynda and Sparky decided to move back to wine country in BC Canada. The Death in the Vineyard series combines two things dear to her heart: Canada and good wine.

Acknowledgements

Writing is a solitary obsession with hours spent creating, considering, and correcting.

However, I have had assistance from some amazing friends whom I have reconnected with since returning to Canada:

- Mary Fry Designs, for the cover of Corked;
- Eric Von Krosigk, wine consultant, for refreshing my memory of lingo and procedures;
- The great folks at Ruby Blues Winery: Prudence Ruby Mahrer owner, Blair Gillingham winemaker, and Sharon Hickey for including me in the Ruby Blues bottling experience;
- Jana Everett Epperson, chef extraordinaire and creator of cookbooks – author of the amusing comment about ice-fishing and homemade ice. Her webpage is at the end of Corked;
- Manuscript proofreaders, Sue Lo, Janice Carlisle Rodgers, and Sharon Hickey. I truly appreciate your helpful suggestions and corrections;
- A special thanks to editor Barbara Manning Grimm, a long-time friend who truly understands the importance of dark chocolate when a writer needs inspiration.

Any and all remaining errors are my responsibility.

There are four other groups of people I would like to thank for their continuing encouragement and support:

- Faithful readers of my blog, A Writer's Life;
- Fans of my two bilingual books for children; The Adventures of Thomas and Sparky;
- Fans of the Isla Mujeres Mystery series;
- Friends from Isla Mujeres and the Okanagan Valley who patiently answered my questions about this and that and everything.

Thank you, thank you, and thank you all!

The legal stuff

The characters and events in this book are purely fictional except the following:

- Jessica Sanderson is a product of my imagination. She was born in BC Canada and shares my off-beat sense of humor, potty mouth, and has a love of critters;
- Mike Lyons is a mix of my husband Lawrie and other treasured friends.
- The snake incident is true, except it was three young guys and three large snakes;
- Carlos Mendoza shares Lawrie's good sense of humor, the love of dancing, plus the appreciation of Rolex watches and expensive cars;
- Yasmin Medina is fictitious, but she is tall with curly hair similar to my friend Yazmin Aguirre;
- *No Regrets Winery and Vineyards* is fictitious. No regrets, no bad memories; was our favorite saying. It seemed like a fitting name for a winery;
- *Loco Lobo Restaurante* is fictitious; it is not based on any particular restaurant.

Corked

Published by Lynda L. Lock
Copyright 2021
Print Copy: ISBN 978-1777-2510-4-8
Electronic Book: ISBN 978-1777-2510-3-1

Hi friends!

Like every self-published writer, I rely heavily on recommendations and reviews to sell my books. If you enjoyed reading *Corked* Book #1 of the Death in the Vineyard series or any of my Isla Mujeres Mystery novels please leave a review on Amazon, Goodreads, Bookbub, Facebook or Twitter. Tell your friends, tell your family, or anyone who will listen. Word of mouth is enormously helpful.

If you come across an annoying blunder, please contact me via one of my social media accounts and I will make it disappear.

Facebook @ Lynda L Lock

Twitter @ Isla Mysteries

Amazon @ Lynda L Lock

Bookbub @ Lynda L Lock

Goodreads @ Lynda L Lock

A Writer's Life

Isla Mujeres Mystery series!

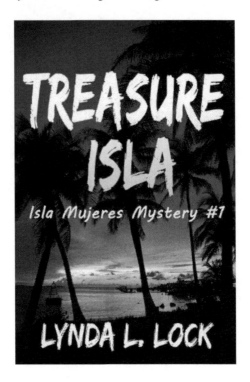

Treasure Isla Book #1

Treasure Isla is a humorous Caribbean adventure set on Isla Mujeres, a tiny island off the eastern coast of Mexico. Two twenty-something women find themselves in possession of a seemingly authentic treasure map, which leads them on a chaotic search for buried treasure while navigating the dangers of too much tequila, disreputable men, and a killer. And there is a dog, a lovable rescue mutt.

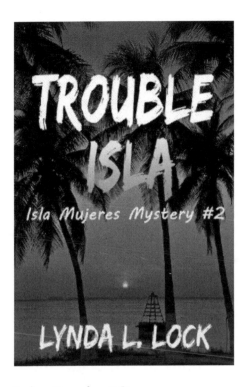

Trouble Isla Book #2

"This pair of leading ladies are fun to immerse in for an afternoon escape. The character development is richly layered and entertaining. The stakes are also enjoyably high, and the action sequences will keep readers voraciously flipping pages. Trouble Isla is a quick, unpredictable read. Bringing this small Caribbean island to life, and populating it with vivid characters that will continue to carry this series forward, Lynda L. Lock has created a uniquely colorful mystery." Self-Publishing Review, ★★★★

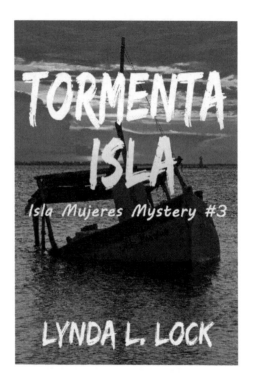

Tormenta Isla Book #3

A mysterious disappearance of a local man and the looming threat of multiple hurricanes headed toward the peaceful Caribbean island of Isla Mujeres creates havoc in the lives of Jessica, her friends and her rescue mutt, Sparky. - Diego held up his smartphone and silently showed her the screen, pointing at the NOAA graphics.

Her eyes opened wide in surprise as she looked at the screen, then a frown crinkled her brow. "Really? Three hurricanes?"

"*Si*," he responded, "Pablo, Rebekah, y Sebastien."

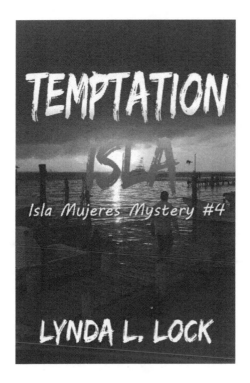

Temptation Isla Book #4

Rafael Fernandez leaned forward resting his elbows on the polished wood, tapping his finger-tips together. "Take them all out! At the reception." He said, sweeping his right hand in a side-ways motion as if he was knocking a pile of papers from his desk to the floor.

"As you wish, Don Rafael." Alfonso Fuentes' jaw muscle twitched with tension.

"You don't agree?" Fernandez snarled.

Alfonso paused momentarily considering his next words. He had to get this exactly right or he would, at the very least, be demoted to the riskiest tasks or in the worse-case scenario killed for insubordination. Depending on Fernandez's mood the flick of a finger or a chin pointed at a victim could quickly end that person's life.

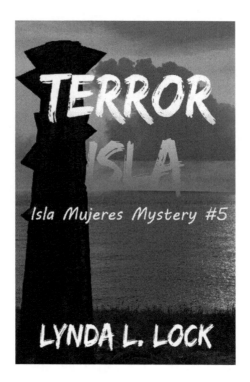

Terror Isla Book #5

Isla Mujeres is rocked by a power struggle between a Mexican cartel and a Romanian gang as they battle for control of the illegitimate ATM skimming. Big changes are coming for Carlos and Yasmin, while Jessica Sanderson fends off an angry lover from her past. Sparky, Jessica's stocky beach mutt is once again at the center of another Sparky-situation.

"I want a super-hero cape. A red one," Diego Avalos said. "I am feeling very underappreciated."

"In Jessica's opinion, Sparky is the super-hero with the red cape. We're just his minions doing his bidding," Pedro rejoined. "I'll pick you up in ten minutes."

Who's going to save who? Join the adventure to find out.

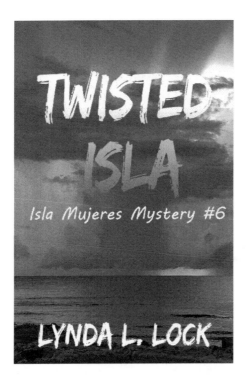

Twisted Isla Book #6

Death stalks the annual Island Time Music Festival. Nashville musicians and songwriters flock to the tropical island of Isla Mujeres to raise funds for the Little Yellow School House. Jessica and her keen-nosed beach-mutt Sparky are thrown into another murder mystery.

Sergeant Ramirez held up his palm with his fingers spread wide, "That's the fifth."

"Fifth what?" Asked Mike Lyons."

"Body," answered Ramirez, his eyes sweeping to Jessica's face, "that we've had to question señorita Sanderson about."

"Really?" Mike lobbed a startled look at Jessica.

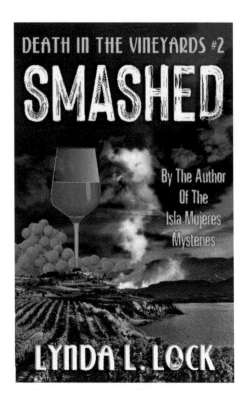

Smashed #2 Death in the Vineyards

Some people can convince themselves they can do no wrong.

While wildfires ravage the Okanagan Valley, Jessica Sanderson and her love interest Mike Lyons, battle to save two wineries; one from the massive wildfire threatening homes and businesses in Okanagan Falls and the other from economic disaster and the sudden death of their winemaker.

In *Smashed*, Jessica and her Mexi-mutt Sparky find themselves in a sticky situation. In this highly-anticipated sequel to *Corked*, inquisitive Jessica and Sparky's amazing nose are again meddling in a police investigation. Will the dynamic duo solve the crime?

Ixchel's Cookbook #2

A collection of recipes from and inspired by the cuisine of Isla Mujeres, Mexico. Over 100 favorite dishes and cocktails from local restaurants and from Jana's kitchen. Learn to make Lobster Eggs Benedict, Cochinita Pibil and bright pink Hibiscus Margaritas.

Try new tastes such as Brisket with a chocolate coffee rub, Pepita Crusted Salmon or Poblano Peppers stuffed with Chicken, Goat Cheese and Corn. Expand your bartending skills with Smokin' Hot Marias, Grapefruit Rosemary Margaritas and Mermaid Mimosas.

Easy-to-follow recipes and options for every taste that will bring back beautiful memories of the sugar white beaches and turquoise sea of our beloved Isla Mujeres. Featuring recipes from Madera Food & Art, Rosa Sirena's, Javi's Cantina, North Garden and more.

Sparky and his writer

34315302R00171